One Soul, Two Bodies

VANESSA OWENS
AND THE
BOND OF SISTERHOOD

BY: DEVONTE COLLINS
ILLUSTRATOR: JOSHUA C. SHERIFF

Vanessa Owens and the Bond of Sisterhood

One Soul, Two Bodies

ISBN-10: 0692871012
ISBN-13: 978-0692871010

For more information, please visit us at: www.vanessaowens.org and feel free to check out our Kindle version of the book and suggest it to a friend. Please and thank you.

CHARACTER BIOS

Vanessa, being the quiet soul that she is, has always been treated with love and compassion her whole life, that is until she met Evangeline. Vanessa is a first year at the magic school, Avalon, and tries her best to unlock her potential. She is very talented but is also quite sensitive to criticism. Her Magica Dominus is Poliy. Vanessa tries to visualize the bright side of life while Poliy only visualizes the perverted side. Truly a match made in heaven....

Poliy is Vanessa's Magica Dominus, or magical protector. He is a cat and loves to shoot out lines that only a pervert would say. His favorite pastime is smoking and checking out the babes. Poliy puts on acts of toughness but as you read more into the story, you'll find out he's quite weak. Even though that's true, he'll do anything for Vanessa.

Evangeline is Vanessa's other half. She is known to be the most talented witch at Avalon. She is a second year at the school. When she first encounters Vanessa, she is immediately drawn to protect her out of fear of her 'condition'. She appears to be cold as ice but some of the students can melt that cold heart and warm her up. Evangeline has a strange type of Magica Dominus, Dominus, an eagle. Evangeline is in great sync with Dominus and seems to be curiously attached to him.

Beverly is Vanessa's best friend. She is also an excellent witch of sorts. She is not very outspoken but she is quite comfortable around Vanessa. Another person she seems to be both friendly toward and scared of is a second-year boy named Jackson. It might just be Vanessa, but she thinks Beverly may have a crush on him.

Jackson is a second-year student at Avalon. He is good at flying on his staff and never uses harsh words or tones. He is one of Evangeline's few friends and notices how much Vanessa looks like her right off of

the bat. Jackson isn't sure what true love is but he suspects that he sees something in Beverly that he likes.

Professor Ludas is the principal of the school, Avalon, and wants nothing more than for his students to grow as individuals but sometimes it's not as easy as it seems with teenage angst combined with magic. He's a minotaur, half human, and half bull; on top of that, he is a highly skilled wizard that is both feared and respected in the magical world. He seems to be Evangeline's guardian and knows something about her that not even Vanessa is aware of. What could it be?

One Soul, Two Bodies

Special Thanks to Bobbie Collins, Janice Collins, Leona Collins, and Ms. Chloe Elkins

CHAPTER I:

MAGICA DOMINUS

Have you ever wondered if witches and wizards were real? Well, they are!

Vanessa rushed through the busy streets of the small and quaint city of Wingston with her friend, Beverly, by her side. Vanessa was a young and energetic thirteen-year-old, Caucasian girl with long brown hair that she kept straight. Usually, regarded as a goodie too shoes, she was always on the up and up and was known as the straight arrow by friends and family. She had a sparkling attitude that encouraged everyone to hover around her whenever possible. She was wearing her usual outfit: a basic blue skirt and white buttoned-down shirt.

Beverly was her best friend. She had curly red hair and freckles all over her face. She was a bit chubby but that never affected her social life; she was always admired for being adorable amongst the

boys at school even though she had never been in a relationship or acknowledged their wondering eyes for that matter.

Oh, and if you're wondering if this is one of those stories about preteen girls in regular schools talking about heartthrobs, you're not quite right but not too far off. There is one thing you probably haven't considered though. Vanessa and Beverly are witches in training. They attend the magical school, Avalon, Institute of the Arcane. Avalon is a school for growing young witches and wizards to participate in classes and understand their powers better. It was first founded about three thousand years ago and has been a proud part of establishing the Magic Community since.

"Oh, I can't wait to get home and pack my book bag," Beverly said cheerfully. She skipped happily down the paved street.

"Me, too," Vanessa said. She suddenly had a terrible thought and slumped to the ground.

"What's wrong with you? Have I done something wrong," Beverly asked. She poked at Vanessa's head.

"No, no. It's just, I haven't even gotten my staff yet," Vanessa explained.

Beverly gasped. "You're so careless! What are you gonna do?"

A staff was a necessary tool for any witch or wizard. It was similar to wands in other stories, and every new student enrolling in any magic school was required to have one before the first day. "She is," Vanessa said. "Wait! What are staffs for anyway?"

"Staffs are used to increase our magic abilities. We can only do so much by ourselves but until we get better, our staffs are extensions of our powers. And we can use them to fly," Beverly explained. Beverly was always the brain of the duo if you haven't noticed by now.

"You know so much; you must be well educated in magical arts," Vanessa said.

"My dad taught me," Beverly said. Beverly's father was a magical school teacher so if his daughter didn't know something, you can believe he was going to educate her.

"Must be nice to learn from your dad," Vanessa said, staring at the ground. She had never known her father. All that her mother would ever tell her about him was that he made one too many mistakes in his life, but Vanessa never understood; doesn't everyone make mistakes?

Beverly put her hands on her hips and frowned at Vanessa. "How many times do I have to tell ya? Chill. You still have your mom and you should know that she is proud to have you; your dad is the one missing out."

Vanessa mustered a smile. She could always count on Beverly to cheer her up. It had been like that since they were little kids; she always knew what to say.

Just then, an alarming type of ring buzzed. It was coming from the watch on Beverly's wrist.

Beverly glared at her pink digital watch. "I have to go," she said.

"Where are you off to," Vanessa asked.

Beverly sighed and looked into the sky. "It's nothing. Just homework."

The sky began to darken and cloud mist surrounded the blue that was left.

"It's getting dark, and I have to go home," Beverly said.

"See you tomorrow then," Vanessa said.

Beverly pointed at her feet and yelled, "Celeritate." A blue spring shot out of her finger into her shoes. She took a deep breath and started running, going faster than the speed of light.

"She is so smart," Vanessa said in envy.

Just then, a red convertible drove up to Vanessa. A tall, professionally dressed woman with brown pigtails stepped out of the car. She had no blemishes at all on her face and she reminded you of a supermodel what with her stick figure. This lady was none other than Vanessa's mother, Ms. Vivian Owens. "Was that Bev," she asked, tilting her sunglasses.

"Yeah," Vanessa answered.

"Was that the spell to enhance speed? Wow," Ms. Owens said in amazement. "Why aren't you that studious?"

Vanessa pouted. She then noticed Ms. Owens was wielding a large, steel cage. "What is that?"

Ms. Owens raised her eyebrow. "Do you really want to see it," she asked.

"Yeah," Vanessa said. She snatched the cage and opened it.

A small, orange and white striped cat emerged from the back of the cage. The cat yawned and looked at Vanessa. He seemed to be safe, so he went back to sleep.

Vanessa looked dumbfounded. "You bought a cat? Why," she asked in confusion. She looked deeper into the cage and saw a rumpled-up tuxedo. "Again why?"

Ms. Owens smirked.

"He's so cute," Vanessa squeaked.

"Horny is more like it," a rugged voice said.

Vanessa suddenly saw smoke coming from the cage.

The cat stood on its two hind legs and held a pipe in its mouth.

"A cat that talks and smokes," Vanessa said.

"Listen, toots, the name's Poliy. I'm a great and powerful Magica Dominus, and I only took this job because your mother asked me to," the cat said in a grown man's voice.

"Magica Dominus?" Vanessa said.

"You see, I bought Poliy to be your Magica Dominus and everyone at school must have one eventually," Ms. Owens explained.

Vanessa scratched her head. "So, we need that and a staff?"

"Did you even read the school list," asked Ms. Owens.

"You still don't understand? A Magica Dominus is a protector that every witch or wizard in training must have. We range from talking animals to even ghosts; in other words, I'll help you with

spells and whatever questions you have when it comes to the magical world in any way that I can," Poliy snapped. "Simple."

"You're simple. Don't you dare get haughty with me," Vanessa shouted. "Mom, where'd you find this guy?"

Ms. Owens chuckled. "He was on craigslist in search of a job, so I figured, why not hire him? You two will make a great team."

Vanessa gasped. "Craigslist? What the heck was he doing on there?"

"Hold on there! What are you gonna give me in return?" Poliy said to Ms. Owens. "Maybe a smooch on the lips!"

Ms. Owens backed away. "Look at the time. Let's go to the magic store."

"So, no one is gonna answer my question as to why a talking cat was on Craigslist, though," Vanessa asked.

"Stand back," Ms. Owens said. She looked in every direction to see if anyone was around and then she held her hand out.

"What's she doing," Vanessa asked.

"A charm is the only way to activate this teleportation spell. This spell sends you straight to the magical world and that's the only place we're going to find your things you need," Poliy explained.

"Oh," Vanessa said.

A yellow, swirling portal appeared. It was rippling with electric energy. It was so strong that it made Vanessa's eye tear up as if she was around onions.

Ms. Owens strolled into the portal and then vanished.

"Where'd she go", Vanessa shuddered.

"Don't be scared. Just step in," Poliy said. He jumped on top of Vanessa's shoulder and yawned.

Vanessa walked into the portal. It felt as though she was in a spa. Everything was warm and tingly. She stepped out of the portal and looked around. She was now in an outside outlet mall.

The mall seemed like an ordinary mall excellent except for the shops. The shops all looked like old warehouses.

Vanessa gasped in awe. She had been to the magical world before, but she had never come to the mall. The mall was filled with people carrying unusual items; one woman was toting what looked like a shrunken head, its flesh shriveled up around its eyelids.

Ms. Owens patted Vanessa on the head.

"This place sure has been remodeled since the last time I saw it," Poliy said.

"Used to look weirded than this," Vanessa asked.

"Weird? This place is a textbook definition of paradise," Poliy scowled. He jumped off of Vanessa's shoulder and strolled over to a cart and grabbed a mall brochure. "Wonder if they still got that manufacturing plant where they make the slave women that'll do anything you want. That place was the bomb." He chuckled.

"Mom, isn't that human trafficking and isn't it wrong?" Vanessa asked.

Poliy shushed her. "Grown folk's business."

"Anyway, let's take a look at that list of yours," Ms. Owens said to Vanessa.

Vanessa dug into her pocket and took out a long piece of paper. The paper unwound all the way down to their feet.

"That's the list? These idiots are going crazy nowadays," Poliy said. He smirked.

"Vanessa, we need to find your staff first," Ms. Owens said. "You and Poliy go find Midgard's Staff Shop, and I'll get everything else."

"That sounds like a plan," Vanessa said.

Ms. Owens took the list and walked off.

"Let's go," Vanessa said. She started down the beautifully cement paved street, taking a quick peek at every shop she passed along the way.

"By the way, do you know any spells," Poliy asked Vanessa, trying to keep up with her.

Vanessa shook her head.

"We'll buy some books for ya, and you'll learn quickly. That's nothing but a bump in the road," Poliy said.

"You're a bump in the road," Vanessa said.

"Nah," Poliy grinned.

CHAPTER II:

THE SILVER WARD

Vanessa walked through the busy mall. Thousands of sweaty people bunched all together pushed her. Vanessa grunted. "These people are going to squish me." She jumped out of the crowd.

"What do you think? It's a bad time of the year to go shopping for your wand and things," Poliy said. "You should really think about being more studious."

Vanessa scowled at Poliy.

Poliy shuddered.

"What's wrong," Vanessa asked.

Poliy looked around. "It's nothing," he said, his voice shaking a bit.

"Sure?"

"Yeah, I'm just a bit cold, that's all," Poliy exclaimed.

"Well, isn't there any way to find this Midgard's place?"

"Let's see," Poliy said. He held his chin with his paw. "I think it's time to show you my powers."

"Huh," Vanessa said. She didn't know this foul -mouthed cat that well, but she was doubtful of his abilities.

Poliy started to glow in a green light. "Sanctum Corpus!"

A green, spellbinding circle appeared below Vanessa and Poliy.

Vanessa suddenly couldn't feel her feet on the ground anymore. She felt as light as a feather; she looked down and noticed that she was floating a few inches above the ground. "Wha- what's happening," she asked.

"This spell makes you intangible so you can now get through this crowd. Now, let's find Midgard's' Staff Shop," Poliy said.

"Awesome. I can't wait 'till I learn that," Vanessa said.

Poliy hopped on Vanessa's shoulder as she floated off.

Vanessa could see everybody as she floated above. They all seemed like dots.

Poily suddenly spotted a small, wooden shack on the edge of the mall's exit. It was Midgard's Staff Shop. "Go down. There it is," he said, pointing.

"Good," Vanessa said. She and Poliy landed on the floor and turned solid again.

The shop was very lack luster and looked like no one had been inside it for years. The outside had not been taken care of and was covered with vines and moss. It had skulls and talismans hung all around the windows of the shack.

"Are you sure this is it?" Vanessa asked with discontent.

"Don't be scared. Go on in," Poliy reassured.

Vanessa took a deep breath and slowly opened the door. As the door creaked open, a low and silent midst fell over Vanessa.

Just then, a giant, fiery claw reached out of the shop and grabbed her.

Vanessa screamed!

"Oh, boy," Poliy said.

"What is going on," Vanessa asked.

"It's just Midgard. There's nothing to be afraid of," Poliy said.

The claw pulled Vanessa and Poliy into the shop. The door closed behind them and the claw suddenly vanished.

"Where'd it go," Vanessa asked.

"You sure ask a lot of questions, kid," a voice said. A small, scrawny elf, no more than about two feet high, appeared. He was green and wore a brown kilt and had a long pointy nose. "So, you're

here to buy a staff, I take it," he said, while tinkering with his golden earring.

"Of course," Poliy said.

Midgard's eyes widened and his cheeks puffed up. "Is that you, Poliy, my old friend," Midgard said.

"Yes", Poliy said in a sweet voice.

The strange elf grabbed Poliy and started strangling him. "Where the hell is my money? I've been waiting for six thousand years!"

"Let go of him," Vanessa yelled.

The elf dropped Poliy. "Kid, this feline owes me more money than I make in five years!"

Vanessa sighed.

Poliy caught his breath. "Look, we came to buy a staff, and I'll pay you too," he said.

"Wait a minute," Vanessa said.

Poliy coughed and whispered, "I'm just playing'em. Once we get your staff, we'll run right on out," he said. "Deal?"

"Okay", Vanessa agreed.

"Midgard, let's get started," Poliy said. He hopped off of Vanessa's shoulder and rubbing her hands together.

"Hmmm," Midgard said. "I've known you for a while, you bastard, and I know you're up to something, but I'll leave it alone just because I don't wanna waste this little girl's time." He walked over to a step ladder and climbed up to a high bookshelf. He started through boxes.

"Excuse me, but what are you looking for," Vanessa asked.

Midgard scratched his head.

"You see, kid, there is a certain staff for everyone and it reacts to everybody differently," Poliy said.

"More than that, every staff has its own personality and chooses its master as well. Try this one, Midgard said. He tossed Vanessa a thin, black staff with clove patterns drawn on it.

Vanessa caught it and stared at Midgard.

Midgard raised his eyebrow. "What the heck are you waiting for? Go on, try it out."

Vanessa flicked it.

Suddenly, Poliy started choking. He fell to the floor, clutching his chest.

"Omg!! I'm so sorry!"

Midgard snatched the staff from Vanessa. "Definitely not for you but jolly good show. Now get up, ya old cunt."

Poliy suddenly regained breath and started breathing shallowly. "Bastard."

Vanessa picked Poliy up and rubbed his back.

"Aha", Midgard said. He picked up a black box and took out a short, silver, metallic stick. The stick was relatively three feet long and had a powerful aura. The tip was crimson. "Try this one." He threw it to Vanessa and she caught it. "Well go on," Midgard said.

"I don't know any spells," Vanessa said.

Midgard sighed and pointed over to a green book that was sitting on a stand.

"A spell book. Go on and pick it up," Poliy said.

Vanessa was nervous. She had never seen a spell book before. "What is it supposed to do?"

"Some spells that are really low level in terms of learning, can be automatically learned as soon as you open it; it was just enchanted by Midgard, probably," Poliy explained.

Vanessa slowly walked over to the book and picked it up.

The spell book quickly opened by itself and a green light surrounded Vanessa.

"I have it. The Rieplum Spell," Vanessa said.

"That spell is used to capture and restrain. Try it out," Midgard said.

Vanessa flicked her staff, and a rumbling sound erupted from around them. Giant, silver chains emerged from the ground and wrapped around a vase.

Vanessa gasped in awe. "Wow!"

"You that amazed?" asked Poliy?

"Well, it's my first time ever using a spell," Vanessa contorted.

"It seems to work well with you. Come with me," Midgard said. He blew his nose with a small piece of tissue and swayed his hand in front of them. A swirling, black entryway appeared.

"Excellent. Follow him, kid," Poliy said.

Vanessa hesitated, but then followed him.

The portal led to a larger warehouse. It seemed like they were on a top floor, and the steel beams were the only things barely holding on.

Poliy looked down over the edge of the floor. "That's one nasty drop".

"Look," Midgard said.

Vanessa looked at him.

Midgard pointed over on the other side. There was a red button emerging from the wall all the way on the other side of the room. "Find a way to hit that button, and I will give you a reward, but you know you have to use your spell."

The floor broke apart, leaving only three steel beams to walk on to reach the other side of the room.

Vanessa gasped.

"It isn't going to be easy," Poliy said.

"So, all I have to do is hit that button," Vanessa asked.

Midgard nodded.

Vanessa noticed a hook on the floor on the other platform. "Reiplum." Chains emerged out of the floor and wrapped around the hook. Vanessa jumped and reached for the chain but her arm wasn't long enough. She slipped and start falling.

"Kid!" Poliy shouted.

Vanessa screamed while she continued to fall through the seemingly endless hole. She saw her life flash before her eyes.

"Use the spell again," Midgard instructed her.

"Rieplum," Vanessa shouted, extending her arm upward.

The chains suddenly extended and flew toward Vanessa and grabbed her, dangling her.

Vanessa started climbing up the chains and reached the top. She sighed in relief.

"That wasn't so bad," Vanessa sighed. "Wish I was more athletic."

"Good job," Midgard said, "but let us see how quick you react when under attack".

Just then, a loud buzzing could be heard.

"What is that," Poliy asked.

A swarm of little blue fairy looking creatures flew around Vanessa. They resembled small humans with wings. They flittered around Vanessa.

"Pixies," Poliy said.

"Vanessa, quickly, hurry to the button. You can't possibly fight them," Midgard shouted.

"Then why did you send them, you maniac," Poliy yelled.

"I want to see what she'd do if disabled and facing down a foe," Midgard explained.

Vanessa started running toward the button, but the pixies started throwing stones at her. Vanessa tripped and fell on the floor. "Is he trying to kill me?"

The pixies flew toward Vanessa.

Vanessa flicked her stick and chains appeared out of the steel beams and wrapped the pixies up.

"Good," Midgard said.

"Yes," Vanessa said. She got up, walked over to the button and pressed it.

Midgard clapped his hands.

Vanessa looked around. "What do I win?"

The floor reappeared, and Vanessa walked back over to Midgard and Poliy.

"You did great, noting less from one of my students," Poliy said, proudly.

"Your prize," Midgard said, tossing a red book to Vanessa.

The book opened and a light spun around Vanessa again. "The Croslap Spell," she said.

"Yes, that is a jinx that sends a light shockwave towards something. It's an offensive spell for starters," Poliy said. "Much too simple for a big-time wizard like myself."

"I present you with your staff, the Silver Ward," Midgard said. He frowned.

Vanessa smiled. "Thanks, but is something wrong" she asked.

"It is just….. that staff has been in this shop for years and only one other person could handle it, but it would not allow her to leave the store with it," Midgard explained. "A blonde about a year ago."

Vanessa looked confused.

"It's nothing, probably. Don't worry about it," Midgard said. "Eh, just take the damn thing; it's on the house cause I like you, kid."

Vanessa jumped in joy.

Poliy gave Vanessa a thumbs up.

"Now about that money," Midgard asked. He looked at Poliy.

Poliy shivered in fear. "You know I'm good for it. I swear."

"Vanessa, if you would allow Poliy and I a moment alone."

A few minutes later, Vanessa had finally made it outside and sat on the steps of the staff shop. She was waiting for Poliy to come out. He was paying Midgard, or at least making up a lie to postpone the payment.

Just then, Ms. Owens came into sight in the usually crowded mall. " Why hello there," she said, cheerfully.

"Mom, where have you been", Vanessa asked.

"I've been getting your supplies," Ms. Owens said.

"Check it out," Vanessa said. She stuck her staff out.

"Beautiful," Ms. Owens said. "Where's Poliy?"

Suddenly, Poliy came flying out of Midgard's shop.

"Stay out, you flea bag," Midgard yelled.

"Poliy grunted. "Why I ought a," he said. He looked at Ms. Owens and Vanessa and his facial expression changed. "He feared me. I had to show him my muscles." He flexed a bit.

"Ooh, what muscles you have," Ms. Owens entertained. She chuckled.

"Mom, I'll meet you at home. I wanna show Beverly something", Vanessa, said.

"Okay, darling," Ms. Owens said.

Vanessa hopped on her staff and it hovered off the ground a bit.

"Now, show me some muscle and help me carry my things to the house," Ms. Owens said to Poliy.

Poliy groaned.

CHAPTER III:

THE FAMILY SPELL

That night in the human world, Beverly was lying in her bed. "I wonder if Vanessa has gotten her stuff yet." She turned over and picked up her flute. Beverly then grabbed her reed and slid it into the flute. She started blowing into it.

Just then, a pebble hit the window from outside.

Beverly sat up. "What the heck?" She got up and walked over to the window. "I wonder what it was", she said. She opened the window.

Vanessa dived down toward the window, nearly falling off of her staff.

Beverly gasped. "I didn't know you could fly! That's so freaking cool!"

"Yep, and this thing actually goes pretty fast," Vanessa said. "I think I almost fell off of it when I flew over the school. Don't wanna have to explain that one."

"Wow, you have a nice staff. Here's mine." Beverly ran over to her bed and grabbed a banana yellow staff with black stripes on it, resembling a cheetah.

"Yours is sooooo much cooler," Vanessa squealed. "That's so cute."

Beverly laughed. "I'll admit it's different if anything else. You ready for tomorrow?"

"I don't know," Vanessa said. She sighed.

"What's wrong," asked Beverly.

"Nothing. Hey, want a ride?"

"Won't you get in trouble," Beverly asked.

"It's not a risk. No one is up this late," Vanessa said.

"Okay, I guess so," Beverly said.

Vanessa landed on the ground and Beverly jumped out of the window and onto the back of the staff.

The staff barely floated off the ground.

"Hey, we're not going anywhere. Is this thing broken?" Beverly asked

Vanessa scratched her head. "Strange. Exactly how much do you weigh?"

"What kind of question is that," Beverly asked. She pulled at Vanessa's hair. "Put all of your strength into it."

Vanessa grunted and accidentally shot Beverly and herself off of the staff and into a pile of nearby garbage. "Sorry. A little too much energy, huh?" She chuckled.

Beverly bent her eyebrows. "No riding expedition, I guess, huh?"

Vanessa laughed. "I guess not." She frowned slightly.

Beverly started pulling on Vanessa's hair again. "Ok, now I know something is wrong with you. What is it?"

Vanessa knew she could trust in Beverly, but this was something that she had never told anyone. "Well…."

Beverly yanked harder.

"Owww!!! Hey, could you like stop, please."

"Tell me," Beverly insisted. She let the captured hair go and folded her arms.

Vanessa twiddled her fingers. She often did this when she was nervous. "Well, have you ever felt like someone is watching you?"

Beverly looked confused. "What do you mean?"

"Sometimes, I feel like someone else is with me when I'm completely alone and I hear voices," Vanessa confided.

"Vanessa, I've never felt like that. That's weird. Have you ever told your mom," Beverly asked? She put her finger on her chin.

Vanessa shook her head. "It's just occasionally and it's not a big deal. Maybe I'm making nothing into something."

Beverly put her hand on Vanessa's shoulder and smiled. "It is still something that should be looked into without a doubt, even in the magical world. Think about telling your mom or researching it."

Vanessa smiled. "Thanks."

Later, Vanessa was on her way home when she felt a strange feeling. She looked around, but nobody was there. "It was faint, but I'm sure I felt it," she said. She tried to not worry about the voice or presence. She had only just started experiencing it when she started looking into her magic history. "I'd better get home now." She ran straight to her house and stood on the doorstep to catch her breath.

Just then, the front door flung open and there was Poliy. He looked at Vanessa as if he were in a daze. He held a beer bottle in his hand.

"Are you drunk," asked Vanessa.

"No, no," Poliy said. It was obvious he was in a stupor state. He threw up all over Vanessa's shoes, green chunks of an unknown substance littering the front step.

Vanessa gasped. "These were expensive!"

"What gave you that idea," Poliy asked. He fell to the floor flat on his face.

"What are we gonna do with you?" Vanessa said. She picked Poliy up and walked into the house. "Mom, I'm home!" The house was a regular, two-bedroom house; it was pretty average in price and taste.

Ms. Owens emerged from a painting on the wall. She seemed like liquid as she came out.

"Whoa! How did you do that," Vanessa shouted.

Poliy shuddered. "Do you mind not talking so loud?"

"You're the one who decided to drink, aren't you," Ms. Owens retorted to Poliy.

"Mom, can you teach me that," Vanessa asked.

Ms. Owens put her finger on her chin. "I can't teach you that one, but I can teach you the family spell."

Vanessa's eyes lit up. "Really! Wait, what does it do?"

"I'll show you," Ms. Owens said.

Vanessa sat Poliy on the couch and followed Ms. Owens out to the back patio. The patio was nice. It had a wooden fence surrounding it so no one could see clearly over it.

"Vanessa, there are five types of spells: Summoning, Jinxes, Restraint jinxes, and Element and Mental magic. Right now, you know Rieplum, a restraint spell and Croslap, the Jinxes spell, but I'm going to teach you the element spell, Windoa," Ms. Owens said.

Vanessa quickly took her staff out. "So I'm guessing Element Magic just relates to fire, water, wind, earth, and lightening?"

"You're catching on quicker." Ms. Owens chuckled. "Bev must be rubbing off on ya."

Vanessa pouted and frowned.

"Anyway, this spell is quite hard and it took your me about three years to completely master it, so I wouldn't be surprised if you have a hard time," Ms. Owens said.

Vanessa smiled. "I can do it, Mom."

"Ok, fly."

"Fly," Vanessa asked. She seemed confused.

"Yes. Doing it on the ground is easy but I'd like to see you perform it in the air," Ms. Owens explained.

Vanessa hopped on her staff and hovered high into the sky. "Hold on. How am I supposed to cast spells?"

"Stick your hand out and say the spell. Recite the spell anywhere near your staff. and it'll happen. Remember, the staff is an extension of your own power."

"Oh," Vanessa said. She took a deep breath.

"Try your best, hun. I mean, you'll never be as good as your dad, but you know," Ms. Owens said. She was trying to make Vanessa do her best.

Vanessa poked her lip out and stuck her arm out. "Windoa."

Suddenly, another person appeared right beside Vanessa in midair. It was hovering without a staff but it was as if it were standing on the ground. It was a perfect clone of Vanessa except for the color of its body; it seemed like a misty counterpart.

Vanessa gasped. "Is that a clone?"

"Sure is. It's a wind clone. Try it again. Make more than one this time."

"Okay," Vanessa said. "Windoa!"

This time, five more near perfect clones of Vanessa appeared in the same fashion.

Vanessa gaped. "This is amazing. I can't believe I'm the one doing this!" Vanessa was so impressed with herself, this being her first real attempt at magic since learning that she was a witch.

"Fine", Ms. Owens chuckled. "Oh, Leo, hun." She snapped her finger and large, fierce lion appeared next to her, its golden brown skinned shinned even in the middle of the night. The lion's mane that covered its entire face was a crisp French fry color and obviously had never seen a brush.

"A summoning," Vanessa said in awe.

"Leo here is my buddy. I've known him for a few decades now".

The lion had a big, bold expression and a pair of black wings sprouted from its back. It roared and hovered off of the ground.

"Decades?! Mom, exactly how old are you," Vanessa asked.

Ms. Owens frowned. "You ready to get a job and move out?"

"No," Vanessa said.

"Then stop asking questions, little duckling." Ms. Owens, like any other woman, was self-conscious about her age.

Vanessa laughed to herself.

"Making clones is one thing but can you use them to attack? Follow the lion and attack with the clones only".

The lion shot off into the sky like a jet. It seemed like it was skating on thin air.

Vanessa gasped. "It's fast". She zoomed after the lion. "I don't know if I can catch up." She could feel the wind affecting her eyes, making it difficult to see. The clear night sky made things a bit better but still not good enough to catch a glimpse of the lion beyond the clouds.

The lion suddenly came into sight.

"Got ya. Windoa!"

Five clones appeared and shot toward the lion.

The lion dodged them and stomped the clones with its massive feet until they vanished one by one.

"Oh, no," Vanessa said. She zoomed around the lion, trying to confuse it.

The lion turned around and shot towards Vanessa.

Vanessa gasped. She nosedived down to escape the lion, but the lion tackled Vanessa. The tackle felt like ton of bricks hitting Vanessa in the back.

Vanessa screamed and fell off her staff, hit her head on a church bell that was hanging nearby, and was knocked out. She continued to fall through the night sky, unconscious.

Suddenly, Vanessa's body glowed in a yellow aura and her arm held itself up. Her staff flew towards her and placed itself in her hand and her trajectory slowed down. She was gently placed on the ground of a nearby park.

CHAPTER IV:

FIRST DAY OF THE TERM

Vanessa awoke the next morning in her warm bed. She groaned and looked over at her clock.

The time was 10:00 a.m.

"Whoa. I've been asleep that long," Vanessa shouted. "Wait, what happened?" She could only remember being hit by the lion and falling out of the sky. She could only imagine her mother saving her.

Ms. Owens suddenly busted through the door holding a blue scarf. "Feeling better?"

"Yeah, thanks," Vanessa said. She felt weird for some reason. Her stomach twisted and turned.

"Oh, honey, you were knocked out. You ought to be well rested for your first day of class," Ms. Owens said.

Vanessa sighed. "What was with that lion yesterday?"

"Who, Leo? He is creature I made a pact with back when I was younger if you're wondering," Ms. Owens said. "Only high-level

witches and wizards can form pacts but it's not for everyone. It requires an intense magical pressure on the user's soul."

Vanessa didn't understand a word of that.

Ms. Owens sighed. "You'll get it later……hopefully."

"By the way, mom, how do you get to Avalon?" She quickly put on her blue jeans and pink tee shirt on and reached for her brush.

Poliy jumped on Vanessa's head. "Interception!"

"Oww," Vanessa said. "Get off, would ya?"

"There is nothing to worry about," Poliy said. He seemed to have recovered from his recent hangover.

"You'll just know," Ms. Owens said. "They come and get you." She walked over to Vanessa's closet and picked up two suitcases.

"Huh."

Just then, a golden envelope with red embroidery appeared. It floated toward Vanessa. It suddenly opened and fiery, boney hand emerged and grabbed Vanessa, her suitcases, and Poliy. The hand resembled the one at Midgard's.

"Oh, well," Ms. Owens said, smiling. "Have a nice trip, hun."

Vanessa screamed as she was pulled into the envelope. Vanessa and Poliy were sent falling down a green, spiral type wormhole.

"Hold on, kid," Poliy said.

Vanessa screamed as the wormhole spit Poliy and her out. They crashed into a steel statue.

Poliy rubbed his head and stood up. "Alright, kid, we made it."

Vanessa looked around. She and Poliy were inside a huge room that seemed to be made of glass. Knight statues and suits of armor stood from corner to corner. Vanessa gasped.

"Pretty awesome, huh? Now what about that welcoming party," asked Poliy. He rubbed his hands together as his mouth watered.

Just then, one suit of armor walked over to Vanessa and pointed its sword at her. "Show me your ticket, young scholar."

"Huh," Vanessa said. She didn't have a ticket.

"Raise your staff," Poliy informed.

Vanessa gulped and raised her staff.

The suit of armor nodded and returned to its normal state.

"Why did that happen," Vanessa asked.

"They just want to make sure you are supposed to be here," Poliy said. He hopped on Vanessa's shoulder. "Your staff is always a representation of you like an id of sorts. Every staff leaves a magical imprint."

Vanessa picked up her suitcases and groaned. "Wish they could have given me more time to say goodbye or at the very least, had less bumpy ride to get here."

"I see we're late, so you'd better find out where your first class is and stop yapping" Poliy said.

"Wait, there's no party," Vanessa asked. Her stomach growled. If there was one thing Vanessa liked more than sleep, it was food. She would make that her favorite pastime if possible. One time, she slept an entire week straight, only getting one form of exercise because it included her going to the bathroom or the fridge.

"That happens tonight once you're sorted into your rooms," Poliy replied.

"I hope I room with Beverly", Vanessa said. "Let's see." She took a folded-up piece of paper out of her pocket and read it. "First period go to Spell Format."

"Head on out," Poliy said.

"I don't know where to go," Vanessa said.

"I can help you with that," an England accented voice said. Vanessa turned around.

A tall, gray haired boy with a very slim figure stood behind Vanessa. He wore a devilish facial expression, while wearing grey colored jacket that contrasted with his dark skin. He stood behind Vanessa, gritting his teeth.

"Hi, there," Vanessa stuttered. "Can you show me where my class is?"

The boy snickered and revealed a black staff decorated with a sharp tip at the end. He pointed it at Vanessa and a light shot out of it and hit her.

Vanessa felt dizzy.

"What's the big idea," Poliy shouted.

"It's all right, Poliy. I know where my classes are now," Vanessa said.

"Huh," Poliy said. "A mental spell?"

"I've done my job," the boy said. He suddenly took a good, long stare at Vanessa and gasped.

"What is it," Vanessa asked. She looked into his jet-black eyes.

Poliy tightened his eyes.

The boy shook his head. "You look so much like someone who goes here."

"Who," Vanessa asked.

"Um, no one. Now hurry to class," the boy said. He folded his arms and frowned at Vanessa.

Vanessa didn't know him, but he seemed to be a friend even though his mean expression.

Poliy clicked Vanessa's ear. "Go," he whispered.

Vanessa nodded and walked off. She hurried up the stairs. Quickly losing sight of the new boy she had just met, she now only focused on getting to her class. The stairs seemed to go on forever in a spiral; as Vanessa climbed them, she noticed many of the suits of armor following her with their eyes. Little fairies and pixies fluttered about on the staircase and stared at Vanessa. She started seeing other students racing about on the staircase.

Minutes later, Vanessa and Poliy entered a classroom in the ball tower, a tower that resembled the top floor of a church. There were only three people including Beverly sitting at tables. The room was set up like any normal classroom except there was no teacher in sight. The room was full of gold trinkets like cups and plates.

Vanessa gasped in awe.

"Welcome to Avalon, kid," Poliy said.

"Vanessa," Beverly said. "I'm glad you found your way."

"You, too," Vanessa said. Vanessa sat next to Beverly.

"Where's the teacher," Poliy asked.

Beverly jumped! "A talking cat!"

Poliy stuck his chest out. "Pretty rare sight, huh?"

"Dad said that you guys are super rare, and super lazy and useless."

Poliy gasped and threw up his middle finger at Beverly.

Vanessa gasped. "Stop." She slapped him on the back of the head. "I'm sorry. He is my Magica Dominus."

Beverly sighed. "Feel sorry for you. And besides, the teacher never came in at all," Beverly replied.

Just then, a whirlwind type wind blew into the classroom. An old, short woman wearing a black funeral dress appeared. She frowned and looked around the classroom, her wrinkles adjusted to the frown.

"Wicked," one boy said.

The old woman gave a nerve-wracking stare to everyone as she waddled across the room. "So, this is my first period class?"

"She's seems a bit headstrong," Poliy whispered.

The old woman took out a long walking stick and cleared her throat. "Now listen and listen well. Before you go into the auditorium to get settled in, I'd like to see that my points are made," she said.

Vanessa's look of excitement changed.

The woman steadily walked around the classroom. "My name is Professor Suna, and I want you all to be in this class every morning on time. Also in my class, we never use fists to fight, so if someone has a disagreement, they will fight with spells. I believe you little bastards should be trained in offensive magic since that's all you ruffians do anyway these days. I swear, back in my day, we could talk even the evilest of demons down and then kick their ass if they got out of line but now, everyone is a pussy."

Vanessa could tell off the bat that this was one teacher she didn't want to cross or be on her naughty list.

"I make myself clear," Pro. Suna asked, her voice booming.

"Yes, ma'am," the class said.

Professor Suna looked at Vanessa. "Are you perhaps Evangeline's sister? You look like her," she said.

"Um, no," Vanessa said. "I don' think so."

Professor Suna rolled her eyes down to her watch. "Okay, you maggots, it's time to go," she said.

The students all lined up, leaving Vanessa and Beverly at the end.

"Hey, hey, hey, who the hell told y'all to get up. Sit ya asses back down and follow orders," Pro. Suna shouted. She started picking her nose with her pinky finger.

The class sat back down, frightened.

Pro. Suna cleared her throat again. "Now, class, line up in an orderly fashion, please," she said in a nice, grandmotherly voice.

"I wonder who this Evangeline is," Vanessa whispered to Beverly as they got back up.

"I've never heard of her," Poliy said.

Vanessa and Beverly traveled quickly down the stairs. "Where is your Magica Dominus, Beverly," Vanessa asked.

"My dad was supposed to find one," Beverly said.

Poliy crawled to the top of Vanessa's head to get a better view. "Hey, I could be your Magica Dominus."

What about me", Vanessa yelled. "You can't do that."

"I'm just fooling with you", Poliy grinned. He pulled out a piece of paper and showed it to Beverly. "But if you want to, here's my info."

Vanessa pouted.

Vanessa and Beverly entered a giant room. The room was filled with hundreds of students and a few teachers. The room was lined with beautiful, frilly wrappings hanging from every side and was teaming with long tables filled with multiple dishes Vanessa had never even seen.

"Fancy", Poliy said. "Call off the search, I think I just found heaven on Earth!"

Vanessa and Beverly sat at a table. Vanessa suddenly spotted the boy she had met before. "Hey," she shouted.

A man with long hair ran up to Vanessa. "Sssh!"

"Sorry," Beverly said.

A short, chubby boy leaned over. "That's just Claus. He is the Time Travel Teacher. Little bit of a stickler for the rules and a rat, I hear."

"Oh," Vanessa said. She really wanted to speak to the boy from the earlier. She never caught his name.

Just then, the room fell an eerie silent.

A half man, half bull appeared and walked onto the stage. He had a bull's lower body and the upper was that of a man's. He seemed quite friendly and intelligent from what Vanessa could see. His gray beard followed him down the long stretch as he galloped. "Quiet," he said. "Welcome to another year at Avalon. I hope you all had a glorious break."

Vanessa leaned over to the chubby kid. "Who is he? Heck, what is he?"

"That's Pro. Ludas, the principal of the school. He's a minotaur."

"Now, I would like to introduce our new students. Please stand," Pro. Ludas said.

All of the first-year students including Vanessa and Beverly stood up. Everyone clapped and they sat down.

Pro. Ludas walked over to a throne sized chair and sat down. Vanessa chuckled.

"Ahh, feels good to sit down. When you get my age, you're lucky if you can feel anything," Pro. Ludas said.

Everyone in the auditorium laughed.

"For all of you who do not know me, I am Professor Aubrey Ludas, the principal of this institution. I'd like to think of myself as a pretty down to Earth person and I'll do anything for my kids, but there are rules I would like you all to abide by. Now, I only have one thing to tell you. No one is to interact with creatures outside the school," Professor Ludas said. "You are able to go outside the school on weekends if you would like. Is this understood?"

Everyone screamed, "Yes."

Professor Ludas smiled. "Eat up." He sipped from a bronze cup he was holding. Before he could barely finish talking, the kids had dug into the food on the plates.

Vanessa took her time, though. She picked up an ice cream sandwich.

"I hope we get roomed together," said Beverly.

Vanessa looked at her and smiled. She turned back around and her ice cream was gone.

Poliy stared at her with puffy cheeks. "I didn't do it," he said, ice cream spilling out.

Vanessa picked him up. "Look here!"

Just then, the boy that talked in an English accent came up to Vanessa. "Hello again," he said.

"Uh, hi," Vanessa said. "Sorry. I didn't catch your name before."

"My name's Jackson Bates. Sorry about that," the boy said. "Not everyone can be lucky enough."

Beverly looked at Jackson and blushed.

"Did you find your class," Jackson asked.

Vanessa nodded. "By the way, who is Evangeline? You mentioned that I looked like someone earlier and now someone else did too."

"She's one of the top students here," Jackson said. "She's at my table, eating."

Vanessa, Poliy, and Beverly looked over and saw her. Across from them was an exact copy of Vanessa. The girl had only one difference: blonde hair. She also had a fierce expression that was totally unlike Vanessa's, but other than that, she was an exact replica.

"My God, she looks exactly like Vanessa," Beverly said in awe.

"She's not the same," Vanessa said. She pouted.

"Yeah, you can see she looks kind of slow", Poliy said.

"Thank you", Vanessa said.

"But she does have a pretty nice rack", Poliy grinned.

Vanessa scoffed.

Suddenly, Evangeline stared at Vanessa. She stood up and walked over to their table.

Vanessa gulped.

Evangeline bowed. "Vanessa, is it? I look forward to seeing you perform well," she said.

Vanessa nodded.

Evangeline walked off.

"Amazing," Jackson said. "She never says a word to anyone."

"I must be that amazing then," Vanessa said. This was a complete anomaly; Vanessa knew nothing about a sister or any relative that attended the school but how could she look exactly like her in every way?

Just then, Professor Ludas stood up. "May I have your attention?"

Everyone in the room sat down and the atmosphere went quiet.

"I would like to introduce the student council president, Evangeline. She will be showing all first years to their rooms," Pro. Ludas exclaimed.

Evangeline stood up. "We have already set your rooms up. Just go into them; I'll show you where they are."

All of the first-year children got up and followed Evangeline up the stairs. When they got to a tower in the very top of the school, they stopped.

"Your room key is your staff," Evangeline said.

"Huh," Vanessa said. Beverly held her blue staff inside the door's keyhole. The door flew open. She and Vanessa went into the room. "Nothing to it."

"It looks like we're the only ones in this room," Vanessa said. The room was an average, room with two queen sized beds and a lamp.

Poliy yawned. "Yeah, yeah. Wake me in the morning," he said. He hopped off of Vanessa's shoulder and into a cozy bed.

The room was quite small but seemed to have enough space for Vanessa and Beverly.

Vanessa sat her suitcases onto the floor. "I'll unpack tomorrow," she said.

"Me, too," Beverly said. "I'm pooped".

Suddenly, they heard loud snoring. They looked at Poliy and chuckled.

CHAPTER V:

BOYS WILL BE GIRLS

The next morning, Vanessa lay awoke in her bed. She hadn't gotten up to get Beverly out of bed. She yawned and started thinking about Evangeline. "Could she be my sister?"

Just then, Poliy sat up on bed and looked at Vanessa. His eyes were droopy; he wiped the crust from his eyes. "What's wrong?"

"I was just thinking, what if Evangeline is my sister or something," Vanessa said.

"That'd be good. She'd be able to teach you very powerful spells," Poliy said. "At least your family isn't a parade of useless drunks. Glad I didn't carry that over."

Vanessa shook her head. "We should hurry up and get to class. Poliy, would you wake Beverly?"

Poliy rushed over to Beverly and shook her.

Beverly slowly opened her eyes. "Time to go already?" She got up and yawned.

In the next twenty minutes, Vanessa and Beverly both got dressed and hurried up to Professor Suna's room. When they got there, they sat in their seats. They were the first and only ones there. The classroom was completely empty. It had an almost eerie feeling.

"I wonder where Professor Suna is," Beverly said.

"I don't know," Vanessa said.

Just then, Jackson walked into the classroom. His expression seemed more lighthearted than yesterday. "Well, hello there," he said. "I thought I was the only one who got up this early."

Beverly smiled.

"Well, you can say we like to be early birds", Vanessa said.

Jackson chuckled. "I see. I went to my class earlier and there was no one there either."

Vanessa and Beverly looked at each other dumbfounded.

"I'll check with Evangeline and see if there is something going on today. I'm new here myself. It's my first year here but I'm a second year," Jackson explained.

"What school did you come from," Beverly asked.

"I was at a private school that my father works at," Jackson replied. "Not for flashy purposes or anything. I don't want you to

think I'm some spoiled rich kid, but I was more so forced to go there." He laughed.

"Don't be," Vanessa said.

Beverly nodded.

"What are you guys gonna do," Jackson asked.

"While we wait on Professor Suna, I'd like to try out this new spell, the Forsythe spell," Beverly said.

"I've heard of it. That spell switches two living being's souls," Jackson said.

Vanessa frowned. "Sounds dangerous." She shuttered.

Jackson looked at Vanessa and laughed. "Are you by any chance, scared?"

Vanessa gulped. "I just don't like trying stuff like that. It's scary. What if she can't put us back right?"

Jackson nodded. "We are in a school full of very capable witches and wizards. I'm sure we will be ok."

"Could I try it on you two," Beverly asked.

"Sure", Vanessa said, "as long you can reverse it."

"Uh, sure," Beverly said.

Vanessa frowned. "I don't like how that sounds."

Beverly held her hand up and closed her eyes. "Forsythe." Beverly's staff lit up and golden sparks flew out of it and hit Vanessa and Jackson.

"Are you all right," Beverly asked.

Vanessa rubbed her head. "I think it did work," she said in Jackson's voice.

Beverly gasped. "Awesome!"

Vanessa started feeling around on her body.

Jackson frowned. "Stop touching there!"

Vanessa laughed. "This is pretty fun, though, to be honest."

"It did work," Jackson said in Vanessa's voice. "Ok, now you can change us back."

Beverly held her staff up but nothing happened. "Uh-oh."

"Uh-oh nothing. You can't change us back?" Vanessa asked.

"It seems you aren't educated enough to switch us back, but luckily, the spell wears off pretty soon," Jackson said. He scratched Vanessa's head.

"I guess we have to go on with school today. I'm glad we stay in homeroom all day," Vanessa said.

"No, we don't," Jackson said.

"What do you mean," Beverly asked.

"This is the day first year kids are partnered up, and you stay with your partner and learn from them," Jackson explained.

Vanessa and Beverly stared at Jackson.

"Sorry. Forgot about that until just now."

"Oh, yeah. My dad told me about that; we get partnered with students that have been here," Beverly said. "It's called Wizard Exchange."

"It just so happens that I'm your partner," Jackson said.

"Who? Me," Beverly asked.

"Yeah, Beverly Collins, right? They picked us last night," Jackson said.

Beverly turned bright red.

Vanessa stared at Beverly. She had never seen her become so flustered when talking to a guy. She turned to Jackson, who was still inside her body. "What about me," she asked.

"You're in for a surprise," Jackson said.

Just then, the room door flung open. Evangeline stepped in.

"Evangeline," Beverly said.

Evangeline looked at Vanessa. "I expect you are ready to go," she said.

"Uh, yeah," Jackson said.

"I feel something strange," Evangeline said. She took out a blue and silver staff and yelled, "Forsythe."

A spark shot out of Vanessa and Jackson. A hurricane of green and blue, clear orbs swirled around.

"What's happening," Beverly asked.

"Their spirits are finding the right bodies," Evangeline explained.

The spirits shot into the two bodies.

Vanessa felt dizzy, and Jackson sat down in a chair.

"How'd you know," Beverly asked.

"I can sense the souls of wizards," Evangeline replied. "It's a little tip I picked up."

"Cool," Beverly said in awe.

"Ugh, thanks," Vanessa said. She kneeled over the gray trash can next to her.

"Yeah," Jackson said. He held his head.

"How did you get like that," Evangeline asked.

"I casted a spell and couldn't undo it," Beverly said, ashamed.

"Oh", Evangeline said, seeming to have no interest. "Vanessa, I want to teach you a spell. Let's go."

Vanessa grunted. Uhm…. Yeah sure. Oh, wait. My staff's in my room," Vanessa said.

Evangeline frowned. Her facial expression turned completely upsetting. "You came to class unprepared?"

Vanessa looked away. "Sorry."

"Go and get it quickly," Evangeline said. She turned her nose up.

"Okay," Vanessa said. She ran out of the room and up the stairs.

"Come on, Beverly. Let's go as well," Jackson said.

"Alright," Beverly said. She jumped to her feet and followed Jackson out.

Minutes later, Vanessa had come back with her staff, and Evangeline led her outside the school to the grounds. The campus was huge. It included sprawling two thousand acres of grassland equipped with tamed animals. The sky was clear and the weather very humid.

Vanessa gasped. "So much space."

"It's not a very impressive sight," Evangeline said.

"Oh," Vanessa said. She felt as if Evangeline didn't think highly of her. Why was she THIS mean to her, though? She didn't even know this girl at all.

Evangeline smirked. "Now look, the spell I will try to teach you is an advanced elemental spell. It is called the Inferio spell," she said. "This spell generates magnetic energy that is around your staff and engulfs it in electric energy." She showed Vanessa her blue and silver staff, crackling with blue electric energy.

"Are you going to show me," Vanessa asked. An overwhelming sense of dread fell over her. Was Evangeline going to try to attack her?

"Not exactly; I'm going to try to hit you with it and if I do, I will not teach you this spell."

"Huh," Vanessa said. She was confused. Beats of sweat fell from Vanessa's forehead.

Evangeline looked at Vanessa. "Inferio." Her staff started crackling with more energy. The staff started shaking in Evangeline's hand. She smirked even harder. "Run."

Vanessa gasped.

Evangeline charged toward Vanessa and swung her staff.

Vanessa leaned backwards and dodged the staff. She fell to the ground and scrapped her wrist on a nearby tree trunk.

Evangeline's staff hovered back to her like a boomerang. "Get up. Sometimes, you must fight others and you damn need to grow up and get some balls and learn how to protect yourself."

Vanessa started to tear up. "Can you be a little easier on me and what did I do to you?"

Evangeline frowned. "Shut up!" She threw her staff again. The staff flew towards Vanessa at about 50 miles per hour. Its crackling electricity started giving off a sound like thousands of birds chirping.

Vanessa gasped and hopped on her staff. Her staff slowly hovered off the ground. "What's wrong with my staff?" The Silver Ward suddenly jetted off into the sky.

"I don't think so," Evangeline said. Her staff struck the end of Vanessa's staff.

Vanessa fell off and crashed into the ground. Her head hit the tree trunk from before; her clothes and hands were covered in fresh mud. She coughed and sat up.

"Got you," Evangeline said with a devilish smile.

CHAPTER VI:

THE DISTANCE BETWEEN THEM

Evangeline jumped over Vanessa and swung at her with her staff again.

Vanessa grabbed her staff and knocked it back.

Evangeline grunted.

Vanessa jumped up into the air. "Rieplum," she yelled.

Chains shot from the ground, but Evangeline jumped out of the way. "I am no fool." She threw her staff and hit Vanessa in the stomach.

Vanessa fell to her knees. Electric power spun throughout her body. "It hurts so bad." She spat up blood.

"You don't deserve to learn this spell; heh, don't push yourself too hard," Evangeline said with a smirk. "Now get up."

Suddenly, Beverly and Jackson walked up to Vanessa and Evangeline. "Hey, what's going on here," Jackson asked, out of breath.

"Why is she on the ground," Beverly shouted.

"We just played a game, no harm done," Evangeline said. "She simply doesn't measure up to my standards." Evangeline walked off.

Beverly rushed over to Vanessa. "Are you all right?"

Vanessa started to have difficulties breathing.

Just then, the three kids heard the sound of hooves. They turned around, and there was Professor Ludas galloping toward them. "Hello, young ones. I didn't expect to see you out here," he said. He suddenly noticed their expressions. "Why so glum?"

Later, Professor Ludas and Vanessa took a stroll to the minotaur's office. Vanessa had told him about what had happened and he was far from upset. Vanessa figured he would be fuming mad.

"I see, but Evangeline only did what was best for you. You must not have been ready," Professor Ludas said. "She's quite a kind person, you know."

Vanessa groaned. "My bruised ribs say otherwise."

Professor Ludas chuckled. "You are so much like Evangeline, it's scary," he said. He opened the door to his office.

"How so," Vanessa asked as she walked in. The office was very dusty and filled with books and giant, black cauldrons.

Professor Ludas kind of ignored the question for a moment and hung his head over a small cauldron. "You know how creatures can use magic just like human wizards? It's just like that, because you're both witches, but the distance between your hearts is different."

"I don't follow," Vanessa said.

Professor Ludas sighed and scratched his head. "You are the same as Evangeline when she first started here, so that's why she is so rough on you, because she wants it to be easy for you."

"Maybe," Vanessa said. "Sir, do you know why we look so similar?"

"Hmmm. I shouldn't be the one to answer that question. Try not to be so mad at Evangeline," Pro. Ludas said. "She comes from a bad past. She never had a family."

Vanessa couldn't believe it. It was sad but still didn't justify Evangeline being so mean to her.

"I'm sure you still don't understand," Professor Ludas said. He reached on to the top shelf of a stand and took down a bottle of blue liquid. He poured it into the cauldron.

"What's that," Vanessa asked. She crossed her eyes over the minotaur's huge body to look.

The liquid started to bubble and fumes emerged from it. The fumes smelled like raw eggs.

Vanessa held her nose. "Ugh. What's that, sir?"

"This is a Chrono Potion that allows us to go back in time. Would you like to see Evangeline?"

"Uh, yeah. Do we drink it?" Vanessa said.

"Yes," Professor Ludas said. He scooped some up in a paper cup and handed it to Vanessa.

Vanessa took it and forcefully drank it. "Yuck. It's sour!" She coughed.

Pro. Ludas chuckled.

Vanessa was suddenly inside a room like her and Beverly's room. "Where am I?"

Suddenly, a younger Evangeline walked through the door. She walked right past Vanessa and went straight to an old, brown chest.

"I guess she can't see me," Vanessa said. She looked at her hands and was shocked to be ghostly again, just like when she was in the staff shop.

"I'm so tired," Evangeline said. She opened the chest, and a furry black rat jumped out of it. "How are you doing, Harold?"

"Fine. You sure are doing good, too," the rat said.

Evangeline took on a sad face.

"I wonder what's the matter," Vanessa wondered.

"I guess I'm doing okay," Evangeline said. She started to cry.

"It'll be okay. Your dad wouldn't want you to be sad," Harold said. He wrapped his long tail around Evangeline's wrist.

Evangeline rubbed her tears away. "Yeah, I know. Dad just told me that I'm not real." Her pale face turned bright red.

"Real?" Vanessa wondered.

"Real? What's real, huh? You're real to me," Harold said. "You're right here."

Evangeline smiled and picked Harold up. "You always make me feel better. How do you do that?"

Harold twitched. "Don't know. One of my many talents."

"Okay, let's go downstairs. Dad is waiting on me."

"Alright," Harold said. He smiled.

"So that's it. She doesn't have a home or a family, does she," Vanessa said, "only her dad."

Evangeline grabbed her chest and walked down stairs with Harold right behind her.

Vanessa followed them and gasped when she got into the front hallway. "Mom!"

There was her mother waiting there. Ms. Owens hugged Evangeline. "Ready to go," she asked. "Your dad is here."

"Yes, ma'am," Evangeline said.

"What? Is she my sister," Vanessa asked? "I never knew. I've got to go now." She looked around. "How do I leave?"

Just then, a feeling came over Vanessa, and she was suddenly back in her room. She was in her bed with Poliy's face hanging over her.

"Are you okay," Poliy asked.

Vanessa sat up. "How'd I get here?"

Beverly was sitting in a chair next to Vanessa. "Professor Ludas had something to do, so we came and got you," she said.

"You guys, I went back in time and saw Evangeline when she was younger," Vanessa shouted.

"Wow. How," Beverly asked.

"Professor Ludas gave me a potion that allowed me to go back in time or something," Vanessa replied.

"Why," Poliy asked.

"Well, you see, I wanted to find out why Evangeline is the way she is now. It's because she doesn't have a family," Vanessa said. "I had no idea."

"Too bad," Poliy said. He folded his arms.

"She was with my mom," Vanessa said.

"She was? You two must be sisters and that explains why you look like her," Beverly said.

"Why wouldn't your mom tell you," Poliy asked.

"I don't know," Vanessa said.

Just then, they heard a loud bawling.

"What was that," Beverly yelled.

"I'll go see," Vanessa said. She hopped out of bed and ran out of the room.

Poliy followed her.

They sped down the corridor until they reached a dead end.

"We'll try the other way," Vanessa said. She tried to move her feet but could not. Her feet felt like they were attached to a ton of lead.

Poliy looked down. "Ew, sludge," he said.

A puddle of black sludge had Vanessa and Poliy stuck to the floor.

"We can't get out," Vanessa said. "Dang! I don't have my staff."

A pair of eyeballs appeared in the sludge. They stared at Vanessa.

"It's alive," Poliy yelled. "It's a monster."

Vanessa suddenly saw a boy laying in the sludge. "A boy. That is who was screaming," she said.

Evangeline suddenly walked around the corner.

"Evangeline," Vanessa said. "Can you help us?"

Evangeline put her hands on her hips. She pointed her staff at the sludge monster and a ball of light came out of the staff and hit it.

The monster gave a low growl and slithered off. "I'm sorry."

"Evangeline," Vanessa said. She slipped and fell on her butt.

"Take that boy to the hospital wing," Evangeline said. She stared at Poliy.

Poliy shivered as she walked off.

"What's wrong," Vanessa asked.

"I don't know, but I've felt those eyes on me before. But where, I don't know."

CHAPTER VII:

A VERY TRUTHFUL CHRISTMAS

Like always, the holidays rushed by quickly, and it was now Christmas Eve and Vanessa had not seen Evangeline at all. The thoughts of Evangeline being her sister stayed in her mind, but Vanessa could finally get the answer she had been searching for, for months. You see, on the holidays like Christmas, students are allowed to go home and then come back after it is over, so Vanessa planned on talking to her mom about Evangeline during that time.

Vanessa sat at a table by herself at breakfast in the cafeteria. She couldn't take her mind off of it.

Suddenly, a water balloon fell on Vanessa's head.

Vanessa jumped up. "What's the big idea?!"

Jackson chuckled behind her holding his backpack. "Sorry, but you looked all sad."

"I did," Vanessa asked. She sat back down.

"What's the matter," Jackson asked.

"Um, nothing. I'm just ready to go home," Vanessa lied.

"I guess I'm not alone, huh," Jackson said. He sat next Vanessa. "How has your first semester?"

"It's pretty fun here. I'm really glad I came. If I hadn't, I wouldn't have met you," Vanessa said.

Jackson gave a thumb up and smiled. "I'm glad I met you guys too. How long have you known Beverly?"

Vanessa's eyes rolled into the back of her head. "Since I was a kid. Why?"

Jackson looked bug eyed at Vanessa. "No reason. Was just asking."

Vanessa laughed. "If I didn't know better, I would say you liked her." Her eyes turned sly.

Jackson waved his hands. "No way," he stuttered.

Vanessa shook her head. "Anyway, have you seen Evangeline," Vanessa asked.

"She went home yesterday," Jackson said. "She doesn't have a family, but I hear she has a nice house on the other side of the world. I guess she just teleports there."

Vanessa gasped. "She has her own house? Cool."

"Hey," Poliy said. He ran into the room. "Vanessa, Ms. Owens is here."

"Huh," Jackson said. "That's strange."

"Why," Vanessa asked.

"Evangeline's last name is Owens," Jackson said.

Poliy knew something was coming. "It's going to be a long night."

"Uh, how about I walk you out," Jackson said.

"But aren't you waiting on your parents, too," Vanessa asked. She really appreciated that Jackson was willing to walk her outside.

I'm not going home. My dad and mom work at the magic council,' Jackson said.

"What's that," Vanessa asked.

"The magic council is a group that oversees the decisions that happen in the magical world," Poliy answered. "They're like the congress and president."

"Those are pretty cool jobs. I bet they're stressful, though," Vanessa said.

"Well, somehow they seem to do it well," Jackson said. "Now go on." He pushed Vanessa out of the door.

"Oh, right," Vanessa said. "Let's hurry." She stormed out of the room.

"Alright. I love the drama," Poliy said. He chased after Vanessa.

Vanessa pushed open the front door and saw her mom standing there.

"Wait," Poliy yelled. He ran into the door. "Oww." He rubbed his nose and felt around for Vanessa's legs.

"Honey, you look great," Ms. Owens said. "Tell me everything that happened."

Vanessa gave a cold stare at Ms. Owens.

"What is wrong," Ms. Owens asked.

"We should ask you the same question! What is wrong you, not telling this poor, poor girl about having a sister," Poliy shouted.

"How do you know," Ms. Owens asked.

"Her name's Evangeline, and she's a student here," Vanessa said.

Ms. Owens sighed. "I suppose it's time to tell you, isn't it?"

"I can't wait to hear this one," Poliy said. He climbed on top of Vanessa's shoulder.

"Vanessa, could we go home and sit down first, then talk," Ms. Owens asked.

"I guess," Vanessa said. She folded her arms and pouted.

Later that night after Vanessa had taken a bath, she sat on her living room's couch and started talking about the friends she had met.

"That sounds wonderful," Ms. Owens said. "I hope I can meet them soon." She sat down in her armchair and started sipping from her teacup.

Poliy suddenly came into the room frisking about happily. "That bath was wonderful. Three months without a bath is not good for a growing, young feline," he said.

Vanessa's beaming expression turned into a cold stare toward Ms. Owens.

Ms. Owens' face turned pale. "You know, I knew it would come about eventually, but there is one important thing I need you to understand," she said, quietly. She sat her cup on the table.

"What is it," Vanessa asked.

"She is not really your sister," Ms. Owens said.

"Huh? But she looks like me," Vanessa said.

"I know," Ms. Owens said. She sighed.

Poliy struggled up onto the wooden table in the center of the room, and poured himself a cup of juice. He burped, and suddenly, his face turned all serious. "I'd like to know why she isn't Vanessa's sister, yet she looks identical to her," he said.

"You see, her birthday was the day she and you were born."

"So, we're twins? But isn't she older than me," Vanessa asked. Ms. Owens cleared her throat. "Your grandpa, uh, accidently used a cloning spell on you, and you can see how Evangeline was made here," Ms. Owens said.

"That's it," Vanessa asked.

"I mean, did you think I was gonna say the stork dropped her off or something," Ms. Owens asked comically.

Vanessa shook her head.

"Well, no, it isn't. The spell book your grandpa was reading from was written wrong. He casted a clone spell and a demon gene spell, and caused Evangeline to be born half-demon."

"Half-demon?" Vanessa said.

"Half-demons are ones born of human and demon parents, but there are spells to change genes into demon genes," Poliy explained.

"But why doesn't she live here with us," Vanessa asked.

"She has been fighting against her demonic side for control over her mind, so when she turned one year's old, we decided to disown her, but your principal took her in," Ms. Owens replied.

"You mean Professor Ludas," Vanessa asked. "Is that who she called dad?"

Ms. Owens stared blankly at Vanessa. She folded her arms. "I feel horrible about sending her off like that. She didn't ask to be born this way."

Vanessa twiddled her fingers frantically. "I feel so bad for her."

"Hey, Vivian, what kind of demon is she," Poliy asked.

"A vampire. Her genetic makeup most likely accelerates her growth and that's the reason she looked so much older than you."

Poliy patted his stomach and sighed. "I thought those eyes were something to be feared."

"I used to visit her when she first started attending Avalon," Ms. Owens exclaimed.

"Oh, but why does she treat me so bad?" Vanessa asked.

"She is terrified and acts out of fear," Ms. Owens said.

Vanessa gasped. "Fear? Why?"

"Deep down inside, she loves you. She wants you to be careful in this world, because if anything happens to you to kill you, she'll slowly die after ward," Ms. Owens added.

"I see. Since Vanessa is the original being, Evangeline's soul is connected to hers and that offers a bond that is almost impossible to break, literally, "Poliy pieced together. "Man, that's pretty sad."

Vanessa couldn't believe what she was hearing. She was basically in charge of someone else's life. Why was this happening to Evangeline? How could Evangeline be shackled to Vanessa. Evangeline was a slave to Vanessa. "She is trying to help me, huh? I'll be sure to thank her when I go back to school," Vanessa said.

"Does that clear up everything," Poliy asked Vanessa.

Vanessa nodded. Maybe it was better for everyone if Vanessa tried to understand Evangeline better and show her that it was ok to open up.

"Now, how about some Christmas dinner," Ms. Owens said, happily. She was trying to lighten up the mood.

"I guess," Vanessa said, darkly.

That night, Poliy strolled through the dark hallways as silence filled the air. He crept into the living room and felt around for the

remote control to the television. "Where could it be," he whispered. "Oh." He felt the remote, pushed a button, and the TV came on.

A picture of a naked girl appeared on the screen.

"Oh, right," Poliy said. "Awesome."

Vanessa suddenly walked into the room. "What are you watching, huh, you pervert," she yelled.

Poliy grunted and quickly switched the channel. The channel switch to a documentary about fish. "What could you possibly mean?"

"Don't make me look stupid," Vanessa said. She put her hands on her hips.

Poliy scratched his head. "Uhm, by the way, what are you doing up?"

"I was thinking about Evangeline. It just doesn't seem fair, does it," Vanessa said. "She is trying to protect me, but if I die, she dies automatically."

"A life for a life. That sure seems like an injustice, although there is nothing we can do about it. Whether we accept it or not, we must follow these rules," Poliy said. "Don't let it worry you, though."

"I just can't stop worrying about it," Vanessa said. "Now go to bed. I'd better not catch you watching that stuff again."

"I won't, believe me," Poliy said.

"Why do I feel like you're lying," Vanessa asked.

"because I am," Poliy whispered.

"What was that," Vanessa asked.

"Do I look like I'd lie," Poliy asked, sweating bullets.

"Right," Vanessa said. She walked out of the room and then suddenly peeped around the corner.

Poliy turned the TV back to that channel with the girls.

"Got ya," Vanessa said.

Poliy shuddered. "The TV flipped by itself," Poliy said.

Vanessa chuckled softly. "Right."

Chapter VIII:
Clipped Feathers

The Christmas holiday went by quite fast, and no matter how hard she tried, Vanessa couldn't take Evangeline's problem off her mind. The next night after Vanessa and Poliy went back to school, Vanessa sat on her bed and informed Beverly.

"Wow, I never knew," Beverly said. "She must be terrified!" She started brushing her hair.

"Well, why wouldn't she be," Poliy asked. "If Vanessa ever dies, she dies."

"That's just horrible," Vanessa said. Beverly could see that Vanessa was beginning to become deeply saddened. "Why dwell on it? Let's go to sleep; we have Time Travel tomorrow," Beverly said. She threw Vanessa a bag of gummy worms. "Your fave."

"Thanks." Vanessa smiled. "Yeah. I'd like to meet our teacher too," Vanessa said. She sighed.

"You're not going to sleep, are you," Beverly asked.

Vanessa sighed again.

"Sorry, Vanessa, but this is for your own good," Beverly said. She held her staff over Vanessa's head. "Easte."

Powdery lights sprinkled over Vanessa, and she slowly closed her eyes and dropped like a rock.

"You put her to sleep," Poliy said.

"I suspect that she deserves a little rest. She didn't rest over the break, did she?" Beverly said.

"Not one bit," Poliy replied. "You know, you should get some too." He yawned and fell to the floor.

"I am," Beverly said. She yawned and walked over to her book bag.

"What is it," Poliy asked.

"Well, I was going to show Vanessa, but when she got here, I got all into her story," Beverly replied.

"Is it important," Poliy asked.

"Of course," Beverly said as she opened the book bag.

A rainbow-colored parrot tumbled out of the book bag. It was noticeable that it was a girl because of its pink ribbon on its head.

"Very lady like," Beverly grinned.

"Ladylike? You stuffed me in a bag for hours," the bird yelled. "I'm lucky that I didn't die."

"Who is this," Poliy asked.

"My Magica Dominus, Grace," Beverly said.

The parrot flew over to Poliy. "What a handsome cat," she said.

Poliy smacked Grace's beak and chuckled. "Hey, girl, you like a hairy chest?"

"Naughty," Grace said.

"Ew. Forget you guys, I'm going to sleep," Beverly said. She got into bed and threw the cover over herself. She cut the light off and then suddenly heard Grace shriek. She turned the lamp back on. "What is it?"

Poliy laid on the floor, sleeping.

"I'm super pissed. He fell asleep in the middle of playing with me!" Grace said.

"Maybe you're boring," Beverly said.

"No way," Grace said. She pouted and flew over and perched on top of the lamp.

The next morning, Vanessa, Jackson, and Beverly were sitting at a table in the dinner room when they noticed Evangeline kept glaring at Vanessa from the other table afar.

Vanessa started sweating. "Will she quit looking at me?"

"You're really feeling it, huh," Beverly asked.

"Sure am. What does she want," Vanessa asked? Vanessa felt as though Evangeline was piercing her soul.

"Perhaps she wants to speak to you," Jackson suggested.

"Maybe," Vanessa agreed, frightened.

"You can get on that right after Time Travel Class. By the way, we should get going," Beverly said.

"Uh, yeah," Vanessa whispered. She and Beverly stood up.

"Have a nice day," Jackson said, while waving and smiling at Beverly.

Beverly blushed and grabbed Vanessa by the arm and ran out of the hall.

Suddenly, about halfway to the top of the stairs, Vanessa looked back and noticed Evangeline following them. She tapped Beverly.

"What does she want," Beverly asked.

"I'm not following you if that is what you're thinking. I only have to go to class," Evangeline said. "As if I would follow you shrimps anywhere." She went ahead and looked back at Vanessa and winked.

"What was that," Beverly asked.

Vanessa smiled. "I don't know but I kinda feel like I don't have to worry anymore. Let's go," she said. She and Beverly hurried up the stairs and to the next floor.

The school, Avalon, had fourteen floors, but luckily, Vanessa and Beverly's class was on the second floor, the floor they were on now.

Beverly suddenly started combing her curly hair back.

Vanessa looked at her. "What's all this then? You were doing it a lot last night too."

"Uhm, nothing. I'm just trying something new, that's all," Beverly said, silently.

Vanessa quietly chuckled.

Just then, Jackson, with his white robe on, floated toward the two girls on a blue staff.

"Hey, Jackson, didn't we just leave you? I think you're stalking us," Vanessa laughed.

"Nawl," Jackson said.

"Fine. You must be heading to flying class or something," Vanessa said.

"As a matter of fact, I am," Jackson said. Jackson peered over to Beverly as she lowered her head. "Beverly," he said.

Beverly looked up.

"Why, you changed your hair; it looks very nice," Jackson said to Beverly.

Beverly blushed fire engine red again and ran into a classroom.

"Did I do something wrong," Jackson asked.

"No. She's just late for class," Vanessa said. She ran into the room as well. She saw that the room was filled with a small group of tables and students, and a door in the back of the room.

Beverly sat at a table with her head down. "Stupid, stupid."

Vanessa walked over to her and flicked Beverly's head gently with her finger. "What is it?"

"I can't tell you," Beverly said.

"I'm older than you, you know, so I'm wiser and can give you some advice," Vanessa said.

Beverly raised her eyebrow. "By one month?"

"Details, details. Now, what is it?"

Suddenly, Vanessa heard a person clear their throat behind her.

A short, blonde haired boy with no blemishes on his face stood there. He was wearing a bold expression along with his ripped jeans and plaid, red shirt. His boots were covered in dirt. "Could you please sit down. We are all waiting for the teacher, who is right outside," the boy said. He had a babyish voice that was contrasted with his face and body.

"Sorry," Vanessa said.

"Yes, you are," a familiar voice said. Claus, a tall, bearded man walked into the classroom. He wore his long, maroon robe and tightly held a stack of books with torn binding. "I planned on the whole class taking a trip back in time to visit the Harpy's Century, but instead, I think you two would do just as well," he said. He suddenly gasped. "Evangeline?!"

"No. I'm Vanessa," Vanessa snapped.

Claus' eyes widen. "Sorry." He cleared his throat. "Well, in any case, Vanessa and young Chad here will go into the past to the Harpy Century and bring back the Glaciem Tempesta spell book," Claus said.

"What is the Harpy Century," Vanessa asked.

"You really are dense, aren't you? The Harpy Century is the century when droves of the demon, Harpy, ran amuck," Chad said. They almost took over the entire region of Fiore about one hundred years ago. Living in the human world could leave you a bit slow, so I'll tell you what a Harpy is if you don't know."

"If you're gonna be like that, I don't wanna know," Vanessa said.

"Harpies are vampires, but unlike in the movies, half demon vampires can roam in sunlight but have hardly any will of their own when a New Moon appears," Chad continued. "The new moon captivates them and their instincts tend to take over."

The kids in the class clapped.

"He's really smart, you know," Beverly picked.

Vanessa grunted.

"You are well informed unlike another witch I know," Claus said. He side eyed Vanessa and gave a blue potion to Chad.

"Chrono potion," Vanessa said.

Claus gasped. "You know what that is?"

Vanessa frowned and folded her arms.

Chad gave a slight chuckle.

"What exactly do we have to do, sir," Vanessa asked.

"Just take the potion and it will teleport you to an instant when the Harpies ran rampant. Just find the spell book I have tossed somewhere in there and come back through the portal I have opened." Claus sneered.

Vanessa gulped.

"Quit standing there, you idiot," Chad said. He poured some of the potion into his mouth.

Vanessa snatched the bottle from Chad and drank some herself. The two kids were suddenly teleported to the base of a mountain. The terrain seemed difficult to navigate through. The sun pierced the clouds and started baking the two.

"We really went back in time," Vanessa said. "Wow."

"Of course, we did. Now, just rely on me to find the spell book," Chad said, seriously.

"Oh, should I?" Vanessa said.

Chad raised his eyebrow. "You think you can do better? You didn't even know what a Harpy was so I assume you can't even fight them."

Vanessa was upset that he was right. She had to rely on him to help her get through this assignment. She started scouting around. "I bet it's at the peak of the mountain," Vanessa said. She got on her staff and started floating upward to the top of the mountain.

Suddenly, Chad looked around and saw two giant, gray bats gliding toward Vanessa. Their fangs drenched with fresh blood. They hadn't noticed Chad but were going after Vanessa. "Look out!"

Vanessa turned around, saw the bats, and gasped. She sped up, but the Harpies were gaining on her.

"I'll handle the Harpy bats," Chad shouted. He unveiled a giant, black, wooden staff from thin air. He started whispering an incantation. Suddenly, chains shot out of the walls of the canyon and at the bats but they swiftly dodged them.

"Rieplum? Dang, he didn't get them though," Vanessa said.

One of the two Harpies opened its mouth and emitted an ear shattering screech.

Vanessa couldn't stand the sound and held her ears, thus taking her hands off of her staff. Her staff started slowing down.

The other Harpy grabbed the tip end of the Silver Ward and slung Vanessa and it.

Vanessa was shooting towards the side of the mountain, her staff dropping into a trench at the bottom of the mountain.

"Goofball!" Chad yelled. "There has to be something I can do." He ran towards Vanessa's staff and started trying to pull it out of the trench.

Vanessa slammed into the mountain and started sliding down the side. She grunted.

The Harpies swooped down towards her with bloodlust in their eyes, ready to quench their thirst.

Chad held up his staff and gray laser beams shot out of it and towards the bats.

The bats dodged the lasers and continued after Vanessa.

"They have me cornered. I can't use spells when I'm this far from my staff," Vanessa thought. She suddenly stopped falling

because she had gotten a slender cliff's edge's grip. The bats split up and zoomed toward Vanessa.

Vanessa gasped.

Chad finally got the Silver Ward out of the trench and hopped on his staff and flew into the air. "Hold on."

One bat kicked Chad in the face and off of his staff, and he fell and crashed to the ground next to a blue spell book.

Chad couldn't move his arm. He grunted. "The book."

"Chad," Vanessa said. She unhooked herself and started falling to the bottom of the mountain again. She held her hand out. "Silver Ward!"

The Silver Ward emerged from Chad's hand and shot towards Vanessa.

Vanessa grabbed it and started riding it down to Chad. "What's wrong?"

"My arm is sprang," Chad replied.

The bats roared, and a dozen or so bats joined them. They shielded the sun completely.

Vanessa gasped. "We can't fight them all with the spells I know. Wait, the spell Evangeline taught me," she said. She stood up.

"What are you going to do," Chad asked.

"Grab the book," Vanessa ordered.

Chad struggled to grab the book.

Vanessa's staff became engulfed in electricity.

Chad gasped. "You're using the Inferio spell?"

"Never used it but this will be as good a time as any," Vanessa smirked. She suddenly felt a strange, swirling energy inside her. It flowed throughout her body and seemed to be charging the power that engulfed the Silver Ward.

Vanessa threw her staff like a boomerang. The staff seemed to cut through the air itself. It tore through all the bats at once; they screeched in agony and started bleeding out of their mouths. Their dead carcasses fell onto the ground.

Vanessa caught her staff as it came back. "I did it, a perfect spell," she cheered. "I can't believe it!"

"I guess you're not as useless as I thought," Chad said.

"Aw, shut up," Vanessa said. "To me, you seem like the one who's useless."

Chad scoffed.

"Get on," Vanessa said. She picked Chad up and they both floated upwards to the door on Vanessa's staff. They opened the door as they flew in and entered the classroom.

The classroom was empty except for Claus. "Good job, you two. I hope you've learned to consider each other's feelings now," he said.

"I guess," Chad said. "If you need me, I'll be in the hospital wing." He got off the staff and walked out of the classroom.

"Vanessa, do you want to know this spell," Claus asked. "I guess Chad was itching to go."

"I'd like that," Vanessa said as she opened the blue spell book. Snowflakes surrounded her. "I know it. This is the elemental spell that encases enemies in an ice shell."

"I look forward to seeing you next time," Claus said.

"Me, too. Where's Beverly," she asked.

"She left already," Claus said.

"Beverly," Vanessa said. She felt good for learning the Inferio spell, but for some reason, she could only worry about Beverly. But little did she know, her mind would be much occupied by much more.

Chapter IX:
The Truth Behind All Truths

A couple of days later, Evangeline sat on top of the roof of the school. She was accompanied by her Magica Dominus, Dominus.

Dominus was a large, white eagle. Its beak was pure yellow and its eyes, a piercing gaze much like Evangeline's.

Evangeline yawned. "I'm so sleepy during the day now." She suddenly felt a sharp pain in her head.

"What is it, master," Dominus asked in a Swedish dialect. His voice was quite deep.

"I sense an evil presence," Evangeline said. "I don't know what it is but it's been here for a while since school started."

"Inside the barrier," Dominus asked. There was protective barrier around the entire school that all the professors put up before the start of every semester to ward off evil.

Evangeline stood up. "I'm probably just being paranoid, but still, I'd better alert the old man," she said, referring to Pro. Ludas.

Dominus stared at Evangeline. He noticed her gritting her teeth. "Is something else wrong?"

Evangeline glared at him and turned up her nose. "Stop acting like my parent or something!"

Dominus said nothing.

Evangeline sighed. "Sorry. It's just that I've been hearing voices and my thirst is coming back."

Dominus sighed. "Kinda hard to get any when your fangs are gone, huh?"

Evangeline nodded. "You know I don't like to hurt people, much less use them to quench my lust for blood." She sighed. "I hate being like this."

"Maybe you should talk to Ludas about it or even that Vanessa girl," Dominus suggested.

"You think so, huh?"

"Stop being a brat and talk to her. It's not her fault that things ended up like this," Dominus said.

Just then, a breeze flew blew through and Evangeline caught a waft of a familiar scent. She quickly turned around and stared into the horizon.

"What," Dominus asked.

"Nothing."

Meanwhile inside the dinner room, Vanessa and Jackson sat at a table eating lunch.

"Where's Beverly," Jackson asked.

"I don't know. She doesn't want to talk to me," Vanessa said.

"This all started the other day. I wonder what happened," Jackson said.

"It sure did, didn't it," Vanessa asked.

A little while later, Evangeline and Dominus had entered Professor Ludas' office but no one was there, so they waited.

Evangeline picked up a clear orb that was on Professor Ludas' desk. It suddenly grew spikes, and Evangeline dropped it. "Damn."

"Master, are you hurt," Dominus asked. He walked over to Evangeline.

"It's all right," Evangeline said. She backed up and bumped into a cauldron.

The cauldron tipped over a bit and some blue liquid spilled out. Dominus sped over to the cauldron and sat it up.

"Thank you," Evangeline said. She peered into the cauldron and the liquid started bubbling. She could see herself in the past talking to Harold, the rat. Her eyes swelled up. The past brought back terrible memories of her lonely childhood, things she would give anything to forget.

Just then, Professor Ludas galloped into the office." Evangeline."

"Who went into my past," Evangeline growled.

"I did. I only wanted to show Vanessa how much you two were alike," Professor Ludas explained. "Don't get mad."

"Why did you do this? You know it hurts to bring up anything about my dad," Evangeline said.

"I'm sorry. I just thought--," Professor Ludas said.

"Who cares what you think? You are not my father," Evangeline yelled. "C'mon, Dominus, we're leaving." She ran out of the office and Dominus followed her.

Professor Suna walked into the office looking completely confused. "Uh, sir, what was that all about, if I may ask?"

"I… is there anything you want," Professor Ludas asked.

"Well, Evangeline waited for you to come back for about an hour and said she felt a demonic aura pass through the school's protective barrier," Professor Suna said. "Come to think of it, I sort of did, too."

Professor Ludas looked away. "I will look into it," he said grimly.

"You're still thinking about Vanessa, aren't you," Professor Suna asked.

"Yes. It just doesn't seem right to deny her the truth of what her and Evangeline's father has become," Professor Ludas said. "I know Vanessa is mad now, but…"

"You mean Evangeline," Professor Suna said.

"That's what I said," Professor replied.

"No, you said Vanessa. When will you realized that even though they have the same parents and their condition, they are different people," Professor Suna snapped.

Professor sighed. "I never knew being a father would be harder than being the principal of a school."

Meanwhile, Vanessa could only think about everyone else around her. She and Jackson were climbing up the stairs on their way

to the hospital wing. Vanessa was very worried about what Beverly was going through, but in any case, there was something else that had to come first.

"It's very nice of you, Vanessa, to be visiting Chad in the hospital even though you don't like him," Jackson said. "Or do you?"

Vanessa scoffed. "I just want to see if he's fine," she said. She opened the door to the hospital.

A brown dwarf walked out. He wore a hat and a green suit. He tipped his hat and went on his way.

"Friendly chap," Jackson said. "Short, though."

Vanessa and Jackson walked into the room, and as soon as they did, Chad sprung out of bed.

The room was covered with yellow, frilly strips.

"How do you feel," Vanessa asked.

Chad nodded.

"What's wrong? Can't talk to a pretty girl," Vanessa asked.

Jackson looked over to the left of him and picked up a bottle. "He took a potion that mends bones, and in return, he can't talk for about a day after," Jackson said.

"His voice, is it gone," Vanessa asked.

"Only for that day," Jackson said.

Vanessa sat on Chad's bed. "Hey, I feel really bad about everything that happened. You wouldn't be here if I were on my stuff."

Chad nodded.

"Wow. Even when you can't talk, you're annoying. Anyway, I'm gonna try to do better so that something like this never happens again." Vanessa stood up.

"Vanessa," Jackson said.

Chad stared at Vanessa and tried to laugh but of course, no sound came out.

Vanessa frowned. "What's that 'pose to mean?"

Chad shook his head.

"Better not be anything, jerk," Vanessa said.

"Even though I love seeing you two fight, you know, we have exams coming up starting tomorrow, so we'd better go back to practice and get some rest in our rooms."

Chad got out of the bed and walked out of the room.

Vanessa and Jackson trailed behind him.

"I think that's a good idea. I can see what Beverly is upset about, too," Vanessa said.

Just then, a raspy voice started booming in Vanessa's head. "Who are you? Are you Evangeline?" it asked.

Vanessa stopped walking and turned around. "Who was that?"

"Who," Jackson asked. "I didn't hear anything."

Suddenly, Professor Suna walked around the corner and noticed Vanessa glaring that way. "Ah, Vanessa. You're exactly the person I wanted to talk to," she said. She walked up to the three children.

"Hello, Professor Suna," Jackson said. "Did you hear something?"

"Can't say that I did," Pro. Suna replied. "Is something the matter?"

Vanessa shook her head.

Professor Suna nodded. "Chad, are you well? It is nice to see you out of the hospital," she said.

Chad nodded.

"You said you wanted to see me," Vanessa asked.

Professor Suna gave a cross look at Vanessa. "Yes," she said. "Come with me."

"Jackson, Chad, I'll see you guys later," Vanessa said.

"Sure," Jackson said.

Chad nodded.

Vanessa and Professor Suna strolled down the hallway and up the stairs.

"Ma'am, if I could ask you, would you tell me what you want," Vanessa asked.

"Look, you know that there are not just creatures in this would but demons also, don't you," Professor Suna asked.

"Demons? You mean, like, the Crisis," Vanessa said.

Professor Suna folded her arms. "Well, yes, that is one. But, you know, the Crisis is not really in the class as demons, but a higher one," she said. Crisis was a nickname given to one of the most powerful but unknown entities lurking in the depths of the underworld.

"I know. I read in a book, and it said that there is no one true devil, but if any person or creature loses their will and trust, they will be confronted by an evil aura and belong to the dark side or something," Vanessa said.

"That's a lie. There is one true evil," Professor Suna said. "And that dark side, it is really that person making a pact with the demon."

"Why are you telling me this," Vanessa asked.

Professor Suna couldn't look Vanessa in the eye.

"Please, tell me," Vanessa urged.

"I think you should really go and talk to Evangeline," Professor Suna said.

"What," Vanessa said. "Why does everyone think they can just bud into our business? This is no one's business but ours!"

"I know, but consider this as advice, not budding into your business," Professor Suna said. "You're not fooling anyone. I know Evangeline wants to talk to you, as well."

"But what was it that you were saying about the devil," Vanessa asked.

"I just want you to know that I know about Evangeline's situation. I just wanted to see if you're familiar with it," Professor Suna said.

"You do? Are you saying she is evil or something?" Vanessa asked.

"Of course not, but her being a demon as well as a witch, may cause problems in her future. Demonic spirits may try to lure her to their side and it would be in her best interest to have someone in her corner," Pro. Suna said. She looked concerned and sounded very motherly. Vanessa had never seen this side of her before.

Vanessa sighed. "I bet that's not it, is it?" She looked over and Professor Suna had disappeared.

The only thing that was left was an eerie silence.

"Amazing," Vanessa said. She had never seen anybody do that, but if her mother could dissolve into a painting, anything was possible.

Just then, Poliy ran up to Vanessa. "I found you," he said.

"Oh, Poliy, where have you been," Vanessa asked.

"No matter. You got to go back your room," Poliy said.

"What's wrong," Vanessa asked.

"It's Beverly," Poliy said. He was out of breath.

"What happened," Vanessa asked. She picked Poliy up and started up the stairs.

"What happened! I don't know," Poliy shouted. "She was acting all weird and making some potion."

"A potion?" Vanessa said. She busted into her room.

Beverly was standing over a small, gray, circular cauldron. "Vanessa," she said.

"Wait, what are you doing," Vanessa asked.

"Hey, look," Poliy said. He pointed at Grace, who was tied to a chair in the corner.

"Grace," Vanessa said. She turned back to Beverly. "What are you doing?"

Beverly started to cry and sniffle.

"I'll go untie Grace," Poliy said. He sprinted over to the chair and cut the yarn with his teeth.

"Vanessa, my heart is beating so fast. Why is it doing that," Beverly said.

Vanessa put her arms around Beverly. "Come on, tell me what's wrong," she said.

Beverly sat down on the bed.

"Why have you been acting so strange," Poliy asked.

"And how dare you tie me to a smelly, old chair," Grace yelled.

"I'm sorry, guys, but it's personal," Beverly said.

"Tell us, please," Vanessa said.

"Okay," Beverly said. "Don't laugh, but I sorta, kinda like Jackson."

"Jackson! That's so cute," Grace shrilled.

"Yeah. I could sort of tell. I mean, you don't hide it too well," Vanessa said.

Beverly blushed and buried her face into her hands. "Is it that obvious?"

"If it makes you feel any better, I think he likes you too," Vanessa said.

Beverly looked at Vanessa. "Really?"

Vanessa nodded.

"But what were you doing with that potion," Poliy asked. He sniffed the cauldron. "Smells sweet."

"It's a love potion," Beverly admitted.

"So we finally know the truth," Vanessa said. "Would you really rather use a potion, than find out if he like you?"

"Wait, I'm not sure," Beverly said. She poured the pink liquid out of the cauldron and into a bottle. "This love spell is used to make him confess his love."

"Then you go for it," Vanessa said, "as long as that's it." She gave a thumbs up.

"Yeah," Grace said. She flapped her wings happily.

Poliy looked uninterested. "I legit thought this was gonna be a revenge potion or something. Who wants a relationship? They always end with bullcrap."

Vanessa and Grace gave Poliy menacing death stares.

"Ok, ok," Poliy said. "Shutting up now!! Are you sure? What if he doesn't like her back," Poliy said.

"Ssh," Vanessa said.

Chapter X:

Crushed Hearts

The end of the school year was fast approaching. That meant exams were murdering the students as well.

Vanessa and Beverly sat in their room. They found it much easier to study by themselves than in Professor Suna's class. Mainly everybody in the room was talking instead of studying, which made it very difficult to concentrate.

Poliy scurried over to Grace, who was sitting at her little tub.

"What do you want," Grace asked.

"Hey, toots, you like a hairy chest," Poliy said.

Beverly chuckled. "Didn't you use that one already?"

Poliy shrugged. "Ran out of material." He kneeled down to Grace. "But if this lovely birdie would give me a night out on the town, I would be happy to stop coming up with them."

Grace kicked Poliy in the face with her stubby foot.

Beverly laughed harder.

"He made you laugh. These days, nothing makes you smile," Vanessa said.

Grace splashed water on Poliy.

Poliy shook it off.

"Hey, Vanessa, I'm having second thoughts," Beverly said.

"About what," Vanessa asked.

Beverly took a bottle from out of her pocket.

"The potion," Vanessa said. "You're not going to use it now, are you?"

"Of course I am," Beverly said. "Now to roll my plan into action."

Just then, Jackson strolled into their room looking all exhausted.

"Right on time," Beverly whispered.

"What's wrong with you, Jackson," Vanessa asked.

"My flying teacher had us do drills ever since this morning," Jackson said as he reached for a chocolate piece on the table. He unwrapped it and threw it into his mouth.

"You must be thirsty too," Beverly said while pouring up a glass of water.

"Oh, yes. Thank you," Jackson said.

Beverly quickly poured the love potion into the water.

The water's color didn't change.

"Cool," Beverly muttered. She handed Jackson the glass.

Jackson drank it. "It's sour!"

"Sorry about that," Beverly said. "That was some of my vitamin water."

"It's cool. Probably need some extra vitamins after that workout," Jackson said, cheerfully.

Poliy jumped on to Vanessa's shoulder. "This isn't a good idea."

"There's nothing I can do," Vanessa whispered.

"Jackson, could I speak to you outside," Beverly asked.

"Sure," Jackson said. He stood up, wobbled for a bit, and followed Beverly out of the room.

"I wonder how it'll go," Grace said.

"I hope she doesn't get too hurt," Poliy said.

"Exactly how do you know he doesn't like her back," Vanessa asked.

Poliy shrugged.

"Anyway, I want to go and find Professor Ludas," Vanessa said.

"Why," Poliy asked.

"I haven't had a chance to talk to Evangeline," Vanessa replied.

"Then you should go find Evangeline, not Ludas," Poliy said.

"While you do that, I'm going to follow Beverly and Jackson," Grace said. She flapped her wings and flew out of the room.

Vanessa walked toward the door when suddenly, Beverly came running back in bawling. She went straight into Vanessa's arms.

"What happened," Poliy asked.

Grace soared into the room. "He said he didn't like her like that."

"Oh, he didn't," Vanessa said.

"I knew I shouldn't have asked him," Beverly cried.

"It'll be okay. He and you can still be friends," Poliy said.

Not knowing how Beverly felt, Vanessa could say nothing. She patted Beverly on the back.

Hours after Beverly had quit crying her eyes out and had fallen asleep, Vanessa quietly ventured downstairs. She had no idea on how to comfort Beverly, but there was one thing she thought of. She walked into the cafeteria to look for Jackson, but found Evangeline and Dominus sitting at a table instead.

Evangeline looked up from her book and smiled. "Come over here," she said.

Vanessa couldn't believe it; Evangeline was actually talking to her. "How are you," she asked Evangeline.

"Fine; better than you by the way you appear," Evangeline said.

Vanessa stared at Dominus, who was not looking at her at all, but was concerned by the dirt clod dirtying his white feather. Dominus suddenly looked at Vanessa. "Good to meet you." He bowed. "It's about time I get to meet this replica of my master."

"Oh, this is my Magica Dominus, Dominus," Evangeline said.

"Your name is Dominus too," Vanessa asked. "Doesn't that mean master?"

Dominus nodded. "Don't laugh."

"You're so proper. I wish Poliy was as nice as you," Vanessa said.

"Poliy?" Evangeline said. "Your Magica Dominus?"

"Yeah! Urgh, he is such a pervert and a liar. He makes me soooo sick," Vanessa yelled.

Evangeline laughed. "Totally not like Dominus."

Vanessa pouted. "Wish I could have a cool guy like yours." She stroked Dominus' wing.

"Let's stop this mystery game. I assume you know about my condition," Evangeline said.

"Yes," Vanessa said. She started to sob. Tears rolling down her face.

"Do not cry. I will always be here to protect you," Evangeline said. She took a hand cloth out and wiped Vanessa's tears away. "I just want you to be able to protect yourself too. Don't worry about me."

Vanessa shook her head. "I can't do that. I don't know you that well but what I do know is that you're a part of me. That's all I need to know to consider you worth my attention."

Evangeline was startled.

"Very considerate, master," Dominus said.

"Evangeline, I always thought you didn't like me," Vanessa said.

"I've always loved you except for that split second when I first met you. I guess I was just a bit rough at first," Evangeline said.

Dominus chuckled. "What's up with the two of you. You are supposed to be at each other's throats one minute and cuddling the next. You truly are sisters."

"Anyway," Evangeline smirked.

"It's fine. Wait, would you like to come and stay with my mom and me over the school year," Vanessa asked.

"I would love that. I have to ask my d…."

"What's wrong," Vanessa asked.

"Did my dad show you my past," Evangeline asked.

"Was that a bad thing," Vanessa asked.

"I hate going back into my past," Evangeline said. She held herself in her arms.

Dominus encased Evangeline in one of his giant wings.

"Why," Vanessa asked.

"You don't need to know. I just had a very rough childhood," Evangeline said.

Dominus patted Vanessa on the head. "Don't you have exams to study for, Evangeline?"

"That's right. Vanessa, I'll talk to you tomorrow, okay," Evangeline said.

Vanessa nodded and steadily walked away from Evangeline with a smile. "She really loves me," she thought. "Evangeline isn't my enemy."

As Vanessa walked up the staircase, Jackson was coming down. "Hey," Vanessa said.

"I already know what you're about to say," Jackson said. He held his hand up.

"You do?" Vanessa said.

"Of course. Weren't you going to ask me about Beverly," Jackson asked.

"Well, yeah," Vanessa said. "I know I can't change your feelings, but could you at least talk to her?"

"I didn't mean to hurt her," Jackson said. "The truth is, I really like her, but I thought she was going to tell me she didn't like me and that I made her feel uncomfortable," Jackson replied.

Vanessa was so surprised that she almost gasped. "I never knew you worried about that," she said.

"I don't know how I could possibly tell her now," Jackson said.

A hundred thoughts suddenly race throughout Vanessa's mind. "I think I have a way. Why not just go up there and tell Beverly really quickly," she said.

"I don't know if I can," Jackson said.

"I'll be there for moral support," Vanessa said. She grabbed Jackson and dragged him up to her room by the collar of his shirt. She peeked through the door.

Beverly was lying in the bed, staring at the wall.

"Okay, she's awake now," Vanessa said.

"This isn't a good idea," Jackson whispered.

"Get in there," Vanessa said. She threw Jackson into the room and locked the door behind.

Beverly gasped. Her face lit up and then quickly dimmed. "What do you want," she asked.

Jackson rolled his eyes to avoid looking Beverly straight into the eyes. "I know I hurt your feeling."

"You sure did," Beverly cried.

"Are you really that upset," Jackson asked.

"What do you think?!"

Vanessa stood outside the door listening.

"I see. Look, you have to realize that I know how you feel," Jackson said.

"How could you," Beverly yelled.

"Because I like you, too," Jackson shouted.

A silence broke out.

"But you told me…"

"I know, but I thought you would reject me. I had no idea you liked me," Jackson revealed.

"Are you sure it isn't the potion," Beverly said.

"What potion," Jackson asked.

"Nothing. It is nothing," Beverly said. She wiped her tears with her blanket.

"Would you like to start over," Jackson asked.

Beverly's face rekindled. "Yes."

Jackson walked over to Beverly and hugged her.

"All well that ends well," Vanessa said.

Chapter XI:

The Field Trip to Hell

While Beverly spent the resting and relaxing days after the exams cuddling up with Jackson, Vanessa had grown a little closer to Evangeline. They had spent a lot of time together and learned more about each other. Within this short period, Vanessa felt she could trust Evangeline with her life. Evangeline did as well, but she didn't show it; she kept a lot of things to herself. Vanessa and Evangeline were sitting on a blanket outside in the meadow, bathing in the sun.

"This is really peaceful and serene," Vanessa said. "It's nice." She stretched.

"Isn't it," Evangeline agreed. "How do you think you did on your exams?"

Vanessa groaned. "Let's not talk about that." Vanessa was always a sparkling bundle of joy but certainly not the sharpest tool in the drawer.

Evangeline chuckled. "I see we do have differences." She gazed into the sky and sighed.

Vanessa looked at her. "What' up?"

Evangeline shook her head. "Just thinking, I have never really just relaxed outside since coming to this school. I was always cooped up in my room when it wasn't flying class or something that required me to go out."

Vanessa smiled. "Well, we're gonna have to change that. When I get done with you, you'll be a free spirit and unhinged just like me."

Evangeline scoffed. "Don't know if I want that much relaxation."

"Hey! Are you making fun of me?"

Evangeline chuckled.

Just then, Evangeline sensed a familiar aura emanating from around them. She quickly sprang to her feet.

"What's wrong," Vanessa asked, concerned.

"Hey, have you been hearing voices?"

Vanessa jumped up. "You too? I thought I was the only one," she said. "I didn't tell anyone because they'd call me silly or make fun of me."

"You're right; they probably would have," Evangeline said. "There might be something wrong. It's not normal to hear voices, even in the magical world."

"Hey, the voice called your name," Vanessa said. She moved closer to Evangeline.

"Really?" Evangeline asked. She frowned and started pondering.

"Yeah. It was if it was looking for you; did yours say my name?"

"No. I think something is looking for me or at least, trying to get my attention," Evangeline said.

"Should we tell Pro. Ludas," Vanessa asked.

Evangeline frowned even harder. "Ugh."

"Huh?" Vanessa said.

"I don't know. I rather not talk to him right now." Evangeline said. She looked very upset. Vanessa didn't know how to comfort her.

"It would probably help if you tell me about your past," Vanessa said.

Evangeline smirked. "Guess I owe you that much, don't I?"

Vanessa pouted and put her hands on her hips.

"You sure like pouting," Evangeline laughed. "But seriously, it is nothing special."

Vanessa continued to stare her down.

Feeling intimidated, Evangeline decided to come clean. "It was just that I remember your mom until I was about one and after that, Pro. Ludas adopted me and took me in."

Vanessa's eyes sparkled. "That's great! He is so cool."

Evangeline scoffed. "He's ok."

"What happened then," Vanessa asked. Vanessa resembled a kid itching to finish a bedtime story.

"Well, I met our actual dad a few times before," Evangeline stated.

Vanessa's eyes widened. "Dad?" Vanessa had never met her dad before. Anytime she would even bring him up, her mother would get quiet, which was extremely unusual for her. You'd think he was dead, the way she talked about him.

"I don't remember his face that well but he used to always visit me before bed and called me 'Eva baby' and I loved that," Evangeline said.

"Aww," Vanessa squealed. "I wish I knew dad."

"You've never met him," Evangeline asked.

Vanessa shook her head. "Never knew anything about him at all. Mom never talked about him and he has never come to see me."

Evangeline frowned. She resisted the urge to cry; it was a terrible feeling to know that he would come visit her but not her actual daughter.

A giant smile emerged from Vanessa's face. "It's ok. Don't worry about it. That isn't your fault."

"Let's just get off that subject," Evangeline said. "Are you excited?"

"About what?" Vanessa asked.

"Professor Suna is taking her class on a field trip, isn't she," Evangeline asked.

"Is she? I must have forgotten," Vanessa said. She chuckled. "The exams must have fried my brain, huh."

"Well, I'm sure she gave you a permission slip," Evangeline said.

"A slip?"

"You have to get it signed by two teachers," Evangeline said.

"Oh, geez, I left my slip in my bag," Vanessa said.

"You guys go today. You'd better go get it signed," Evangeline said.

Vanessa got to her feet and ran inside the school. Almost tackling everyone, she made it to her room door and held her staff up and the door magically opened. She ran to her bag and pried it open.

The permission slip was at the bottom and was wrapped in scarlet paper.

Vanessa snatched it out and hurried out of the room. She raced to Professor Suna's classroom to find the door closed and locked. "No!"

Suddenly, Jackson, who was strolling down the hall, appeared, and noticed a depressed Vanessa. "What is wrong?"

Vanessa looked up. "I missed my trip," she replied.

"For who," Jackson asked.

"Professor Suna," Vanessa said. She hung her head down.

"No you didn't. Beverly is outside by the portal with rest of the class waiting for you," Jackson said, in what seemed to be a serious voice.

"Really? They haven't left," Vanessa asked. Color returned to her face.

"No fooling," Jackson said. "Hurry up."

Vanessa rushed down the staircase, almost tripping over her shoelaces. She busted outside into the meadow, which she saw everyone was standing there just as Jackson had assured but they had boiling mad looks on their faces.

"You!" the kids yelled.

"Glad to see you, Ms. Owens," Professor Suna said. The motherly expression from before was surely gone now.

"I'm so sorry," Vanessa said, panting.

"Sure, I know you are," Professor Suna said.

The kids burst out in joyful laughter now. With their horrible expressions gone, Vanessa knew it was safe to approach them.

Beverly waved her arm as Vanessa walked over to her.

"As I was saying, I am about to create another wormhole for each of you," Professor Suna barked. "A wormhole is a direct transportation device to wherever you may want to go. I'm sure you all remember the wormhole used to teleport you to the school before."

"Where are we going, ma'am," Vanessa asked.

Pro. Suna smirked. "If you had come on time, you would know that we are taking a trip to Hell."

"Hell?" Vanessa shrieked. "Is that safe?"

"Typically, no, but I will assure you, you will be fine. But that is the reason I gave you all the permission slips before the Christmas break. I wanted parent consent," Pro. Suna barked.

"Right," Vanessa said, disheartened. She noticed that her slip wasn't signed. She had spent so much time moping over Evangeline at that time.

"So, what took you so long," Beverly whispered.

"I couldn't find my slip," Vanessa said. She held the colorful slip of paper up.

"It's not signed," Beverly said.

"Oh, no. I can't go."

"Hush up," Professor Suna yelled.

Vanessa simply didn't hear her and kept yammering to Beverly, who had quit talking and nodded to everything she said.

Professor Suna flicked her staff and a blue, green swirling portal appeared. A strong suction emitted from the portal. It almost picked Beverly up right off her feet.

"That's really strong," Beverly said.

"Thanks for pointing out the obvious" one girl snapped.

Beverly gave a stern look at the girl.

Just then, the permission slip flew out of Vanessa's hand and into the portal.

Vanessa gasped.

"An unfortunate event, your slip going into the portal; it could be anywhere now. I guess I must automatically let you attend the trip," Professor Suna said.

Vanessa considered herself lucky. She hadn't gotten the slip signed at all and Professor Suna didn't know that. Vanessa wouldn't say anything but left it as that.

"You will be partnered up and use the wormhole. Beverly, you shall accompany Vanessa," Professor Suna said. "I'm sure I can trust you to keep her safe."

"Yes, ma'am," Beverly said.

Vanessa scoffed. "I'm not that bad."

"Every one of you will be teleported to a closed off part of Hell where no demons can get to. They should not be able to penetrate the

force field we have around the section. Now go and explore the depths of Hell but be back in about 30 minutes."

"Let's go," Vanessa said. She and Beverly walked into the wormhole and disappeared.

"Ugh, I didn't check Beverly's slip. I seem to be slipping," Professor Suna said.

Vanessa and Beverly stepped out into a dark cave. It was not pitch black; there were lanterns setup through a walk way. "It's so hot in here."

"Don't worry about that. It's too dark in here," Beverly said. She held her staff up and it started to glow enough to illuminate their surroundings.

Vanessa smiled and looked across the cavern. She spotted boiling lava spewing from the ground. "Is this a volcano or something?"

"Hell is a part of the underworld and is known to possess lava that comes out of the cracks in the walls. That's probably why it's so hot."

"So, what are we here for exactly?"

"Just to get a firsthand look at Hell. All we've done is read about it before. I'm kinda excited honestly," Beverly replied.

Vanessa grunted. "Who sends their class to Hell anyway?"

Beverly chuckled. "Right?"

"First, we have to get across the lava that is coming out of the ground," Vanessa said.

"Try the Icy Wind spell," Beverly said.

Vanessa pointed her staff at the lava and a powdery substance spewed out and turned the lava into hard as rock ice. "I did it."

"Let's get across before it melts," Beverly said. She and Vanessa hurried across the sliding ice and into the passage. It led to a long tunnel which was still as dark as the clearing before it. "Someone's been down here," Beverly said.

"Should we go on," Vanessa asked.

"Of course. If we run into trouble, I'll just use the wormhole," Beverly reassured.

Vanessa suddenly heard a low growl and turned around quickly. It came from the frozen lava, or lava, because it was melting.

"It melted so fast," Beverly said. "I shouldn't be so surprised I heard this lava is no less than one thousand degrees."

Vanessa looked into the lava and saw a figure move inside it. "Beverly."

Beverly stared into the lava and noticed it, too. "What is that?"

Just then, a giant, black, stone gargoyle emerged from the lava and roared. It was standing a whopping eight feet tall and its wings were at least five feet wide. Lava spewed from its mouth.

"What the heck," Vanessa yelled. "I thought there were no monsters."

"That's a creature in Hell, a gargoyle. Professor Suna told us that we had to kill one and bring its wing back for a grade," Beverly said.

"And you're telling me this now," Vanessa asked.

"I forgot," Beverly shouted.

The gargoyle spread its wings open and flew toward the girls after hovering in the air for a couple of seconds.

"We can handle it, if we work together," Vanessa said. "Rieplum!" Chains appeared and wrapped tightly around the gargoyle's throat.

"Will it choke it," Beverly asked.

The gargoyle broke free and shot toward the girls once again. It dived and grabbed Beverly in its claws and carried her through the tunnel.

"Beverly," Vanessa yelled. She chased after them down the tunnel.

The gargoyle stopped inside a huge room and glided above a giant, yellow orb. The orb was being held from the ceiling by a group of large chains.

"What's that," Vanessa wondered.

"Vanessa," Beverly yelled. She became dizzy and could feel the blood rushing to her head.

"Oh, right,", Vanessa said.

The gargoyle dived down toward Vanessa and threw Beverly.

Beverly fell onto Vanessa, pushing her down. Vanessa fell over the little cliff and landed on the yellow orb. "Ow," she said.

The gargoyle flew toward Vanessa with its large mouth wide open.

"Look out," Beverly yelled.

Vanessa held her staff up. "There's only one thing to do. Inferio!" She threw her staff, which was engulfed in electricity, like a boomerang.

The gargoyle tried to dodge it but its wing was struck and got chopped off. Green blood spewed out. The wing landed beside Beverly whiled the gargoyle fell to the ground and went into a frenzy. It stood back up and hovered towards Beverly.

Beverly gasped. "It's still up?"

Vanessa grunted and jumped onto her staff and flew towards the gargoyle.

The gargoyle pointed its remaining wing towards Vanessa. The wing detached from its body and flew towards her.

"What," Beverly yelled. "Don't touch it, Vanessa. It will explode."

Vanessa gasped and dived downward to avoid the wing. The wing crashed into the chains holding the orb up and exploded, destroying two of the chains. The orb was left hanging at an angle.

"You did it," Beverly said.

"Don't celebrate yet," Vanessa said.

The gargoyle, now wingless, fell to the ground. It twitched and struggled to get up but could not.

Vanessa landed next to Beverly.

"I'm glad that's over. Let's go, 'nessa," Beverly said. She flicked her staff and a wormhole opened.

"Wait. I wanna check this orb out," Vanessa said. "The stupid gargoyle messed it up. Its hanging."

"But what if another one comes," Beverly asked.

"It'll only take a second," Vanessa replied, flying back to the orb.

Beverly began tapping her foot impatiently.

Vanessa started examining the ball that she stood one. She couldn't find a way to open it. "I wonder what it is." She tapped the ball with her staff and the orb dimmed.

"Vanessa, what did you do," Beverly asked.

"Nothing!" Vanessa's staff started changing, taking new form. It changed into a long, silver and metal staff with a star on top of it.

"Finally, I can take shape," a voice boomed.

Vanessa looked around. It was the same voice she was too familiar with.

"What just happened," Beverly asked. "Vanessa, come on," Beverly said.

Vanessa was confounded. Why did her staff just change? True enough, Vanessa liked the improved star on top but still.

"Your staff has changed," Beverly said. "You've got to tell Professor Suna."

Vanessa suddenly felt an overwhelming power coming from the staff. It was similar to Vanessa's own magical pressure but it was like someone else's was now mixed in with it. She flew back down to Beverly. "I'll talk to Jackson, okay?"

"You promise," Beverly asked.

Vanessa didn't say a word. She walked in through the wormhole with Beverly following behind her. They came out inside Professor Suna's classroom to find half the class there. The hole closed as Beverly dragged the end of the wing through.

Professor Suna was sitting at her desk. "Very nice. A simple task even Owens can complete," she said.

Vanessa groaned while the classroom filled with laughter.

"A fine specimen you have brought," Professor Suna congratulated.

"Right," Beverly said, helping Vanessa hide her staff behind their backs.

"You can go to your room, if you want," Professor Suna said. "Class is over with. I just need to wait on a few others."

"Good," Vanessa said. She and Beverly hurried out of the room and out the door.

Beverly sighed as they walked up the staircase.

Vanessa scratched her head. "Where is Jackson?"

"I don't know," Beverly said.

Vanessa sighed. She was still worried about the voices she had been hearing. She hadn't heard that voice in months but why come back now?

Chapter XII:

Magic Outside the Classroom

With January coming to a close, Vanessa couldn't wait to go home with her sister, Evangeline, but the last days didn't go by so smooth. When Vanessa found out that Jackson was taking a special test, she was quite mad. Her questions about her staff would remain unanswered. Today, she and Poliy sat in the abandoned classroom examining the staff.

"I've never seen this," Poliy said.

"It feels the same sorta," Vanessa said.

"Why sorta," Poliy asked.

"It feels like there are two different energies in it," Vanessa explained. "Like, I feel my magical pressure but someone else's too."

Magical pressure was the certain imprint that every witch and wizard gave off.

"Maybe you could ask Evangeline," Poliy said.

"She's taking that test, too," Vanessa replied.

"Well, we should at least find out how it works. Try something," Poliy said.

Vanessa waved her staff but nothing happened.

"That was a dud," Poliy said. "You couldn't have lost your magic, could you?"

Vanessa shrugged. She waved her staff again and it shot a light at the wall.

"The Croslap spell, you can still use it," Poliy said.

"I don't understand," Vanessa said. She groaned and slammed her head on the table.

"By the way, has Beverly come back yet," Poliy asked.

"No. She's still in the library looking for some info on the staff," Vanessa said.

"Cool," Poliy said. "Let's go and get her then."

"Alright," Vanessa said. She and Poliy slowly crept out of the classroom and down the hall until they got to a huge, bronze door. Vanessa pushed the door open so Poliy could hurry in after her.

The library was so quiet, you could hear a pin drop. Like any library, there were books everywhere but this one was huge, like a maze.

"We'll never find our way through this," Vanessa said.

"Not without this," Poliy said. He pointed at a pink book on a stand. "It's a spell book. They must keep in here for some reason."

Vanessa tapped the book with her hand and a pink light surrounded her. "The Transcro Spell."

"That's a guiding spell. Good," Poliy said.

"Transcro," Vanessa shouted. A thick trial of yellow light appeared and seemed to lead deeper into the library.

"That light will lead us to Beverly," Poliy said.

Vanessa and Poliy followed the strip of light through sections of the somewhat mystical maze.

The strip stopped at the very back of the library.

"Where is she," Poliy asked.

"Here," Beverly said. She was under the table.

"What are you doing," Vanessa asked.

Beverly's eyes grew big. She jumped on Vanessa! "Vanessa, we have to do something."

"What," Vanessa asked.

Beverly showed Vanessa and Poliy a blue, old book. "This book says the orb you were on is called the Drainage. Your staff drained its power somehow and that's what made it change," she yelled.

"Ssh," Vanessa said. She took Beverly over to the corner.

"Tell us more," Poliy said to Beverly.

"The Silver Ward is being draining the Drainage's magical prowess," Beverly said. "There's nothing we can do about Vanessa's staff's form, but we have to find some way to separate the Drainage and the staff."

"That must be your staff's ability" Poliy said.

"Ability?" Vanessa said.

"I have never read about a staff having a power on its own," Beverly said.

"Yeah. Some staves have their own wills and abilities. Seems the Silver Ward has the power to drain magical pressure but it chose the wrong one this time. The Drainage is a parasitic item from Hell that allowed the Silver Ward to suck it in," Poliy explained.

"Allowed," Vanessa said. "What are you talking about?"

"The Drainage is going to slowly suck your magical prowess away. It probably changed the staff's appearance to deceive us," Beverly added.

Vanessa gasped. "How do we separate them? The book tells you how to do it, right," Vanessa asked.

"No," Beverly said.

"Are you sure there's not anything at all," Poliy asked.

"Think, Beverly," Vanessa shouted.

"I am," Beverly yelled, panicking. "Wait. Why can you still cast spells then?" She flipped to a page in the book.

"I don't know," Vanessa said. "When I cast spells, it doesn't feel like me though."

"What could it be," Poliy asked.

Just then, the door they can in through closed.

"Someone came in," Beverly whispered.

"We have to hide," Vanessa said.

"Quick," Poliy said. He tripped over his foot and bumped into Beverly. He pushed her and he and her both fell down a laundry chute that was behind Vanessa.

Vanessa heard the heavy footsteps grow closer. She grabbed the blue book and hid behind the nearest bookshelf she could find.

The footsteps came to a halt.

Vanessa peeped around the bookshelf, and there were two people standing there: Professor Suna and an old woman wearing beads and an ancient, blue dress. Vanessa believed the other woman to be the librarian, Ms. Norris.

Ms. Norris gave a grim look at Professor Suna.

"What did you want me for," Professor Suna asked.

"I am missing a bottle of vampire breath," Ms. Norris exclaimed.

"And?" Professor Suna smirked.

"Have you been using it to teach your students again," Ms. Norris asked.

"No. I haven't even been to the library all year; why, vampire teaching isn't even on the agenda this year," Professor Suna replied.

"I've no idea where it is. I couldn't have misplaced it, it's so valuable," Ms. Norris said.

"May I ask what is so valuable about it," Professor Suna asked.

"Professor Ludas gave it to me. It is E--," Ms. Norris said, but before she could finish, Vanessa had dropped the book and it made a loud thud. Surely, it caught Ms. Norris' and Professor Suna's attention.

"Who is there," Professor Suna demanded.

Vanessa stepped out from behind the bookshelf.

"What are you doing here, nosy misfit," Professor Suna asked.

"I was checking out a book, but Ms. Norris wasn't here," Vanessa said, trying to quickly pick up the book she had dropped.

Ms. Norris noticed the book. "Give me that."

Vanessa handed her the book. Unfortunately, it was on the page about the Drainage.

Ms. Norris showed Professor Suna the book.

Professor Suna stared at Vanessa. "What are you looking for in this book?"

"I only just picked it up," Vanessa lied, trying not to crack a grin.

"You sure," Ms. Norris asked.

Vanessa gulped.

Professor Suna took a short, green staff out and waved it over Vanessa's head. She sneezed.

"Now tell me, why do you have this book," Professor said.

Vanessa couldn't control her words. "I was looking for a way to separate the Drainage from my staff."

Profess Suna nodded. "Show me the staff."

Vanessa held her staff out. The staff had turned from silver to black. "It has almost taken your power. I'm sure you got infected when you were in Hell; you should have told me," Professor Suna said.

"Hold on. Have you been the one stealing my breath," Ms. Norris asked.

Vanessa shook her head.

Ms. Norris sighed.

Professor Suna dug into her pocket and pulled out a slip of paper. "A talisman should fix this. The Drainage has not completely taken over the staff." She placed it on Vanessa's staff and at that moment, Vanessa felt like a heavy burden had been lifted off of her. She noticed her staff changed back to being silver but still had the star on the top of it.

"I bet that feels better," Professor said.

"Sure does," Vanessa said. "Thank you, ma'am."

"You're not off the hook yet," Professor Suna said.

"Huh," Vanessa said.

"You did not tell me about this sooner. That is a complete lack of trust and it's against the rules. I'm sorry, but you have detention on tomorrow," Professor Suna said.

"What," Vanessa shouted.

"Do you want two," Professor Suna asked.

"No, ma'am," Vanessa muttered.

"Then lower your voice when talking to me," Professor Suna snapped.

Vanessa sighed sharply.

"I should report this to Professor Ludas, but I won't, seeing as this is your first time getting into trouble," Professor Suna said.

"You're very generous," Ms. Norris said.

"I know I am," Professor Suna said. "Now come on, Vanessa, let's go to the dinner room before all of the cakes are gone." She and Vanessa started out the door.

"Hey, try and find that breath, okay," Ms. Norris yelled.

"Yeah, yeah," Professor Suna said weakly.

"Bitch," Ms. Norris said under her breath.

Just then, a blast of light shot out of the laundry chute and hit her on the butt. Ms. Norris jumped! She didn't wonder about it; she just backed away slowly.

Chapter XIII:

Detention with Claus

Later that night after Professor Suna had cleared the Drainage spell from Vanessa's staff, Vanessa, Grace, and Poliy rested in Vanessa and Beverly's room. Vanessa felt much relief since then, even if it was, like, about two hours earlier.

Poliy jumped on to the bed. "I'm glad Professor Suna got rid of that curse. I was worried," he said.

"You guys never tell me anything," Grace yelled.

"You were gone somewhere; it's not our fault," Vanessa retorted.

Grace pouted and flew over to her little tub.

Beverly came into the room and sighed as she sat on her bed. "I'm so glad you were able to get that Drainage off the staff," she said.

"But it still looks the same," Poliy said.

"It'll be okay, I guess," Vanessa said. She yawned. "It's still the Silver Ward."

"I can't believe you got detention though," Beverly said.

"Yeah, yeah," Vanessa said wearily.

"You better get going," Beverly said.

"You have detention at night," Poliy asked Vanessa.

"Yeah." Vanessa got up and walked toward the door. She opened it and waved as she went into the hallway. She walked slowly down the stairs. She didn't want to go, but maybe since it was a two hour detention, the person giving detention would let her go early. Vanessa went straight to Professor Suna's door and stood there.

Just then, Claus appeared and tightly grabbed her hand.

Vanessa grunted. "Hey."

"I am in charge of detention and Professor Suna has informed me that you were coming," Claus said. "Come with me."

Vanessa held her what seemed to be a broken wrist, and followed Claus outside into the meadow. They were walking around to the back of the school.

"So tell me, Owens, what are ye in for," Claus said.

"I raised my voice at Professor Suna," Vanessa said.

"Are you sure? She would've handled that, not with detention, though," Claus said. "It's funny how you guys have detention on the last week of school. Quite stupid, actually, don't you think?"

"You mean, someone else is here," Vanessa said.

"Yeah, a boy. Chad, I think," Claus replied.

"Where is he," Vanessa asked.

"He's waiting for me," Claus said. He and Vanessa stopped by a long, iron gate. "Come out, boy."

Chad suddenly appeared in front of them.

"Where'd he come from," Vanessa asked.

"I told the boy to camouflage himself; he's quite smart. You know, I wouldn't want any creature out here to eat ya," Claus said.

"You like us," Vanessa said, dreamily.

"Hell no! If something happened to you, I'd be out of a job," Claus said. "Now come on."

Chad and Vanessa followed Claus into a forest through the iron gates. "Why are we here," Chad asked.

"This is your detention. There's been some damn beast feeding on our livestock, and I'm gonna find out what and you're going to help," Claus replied.

"A monster," Chad said.

"It is quite funny. The beast comes only on the New Moon and there's one this whole week," Claus said.

"So you've got four more tries if you don't get it today," Vanessa said.

"Right," Claus said.

"What's missing from the livestock," Chad asked.

"Blood," Claus said.

"Blood and the New Moon. That sounds like a Harpy," Chad said.

"No. We carry creatures, but not vampires," Claus said.

Just then, there was a sound of rustling leaves.

"What was that," Vanessa asked.

"Stay on your guard," Claus ordered.

Suddenly, the air around them got much colder.

"I feel strange," Chad said.

"Heh, you'd hate to go back to the hospital, huh," Vanessa said.

Claus suddenly saw a figure jumping from tree to tree. "Die." He took his gray staff out and started shooting green rays of light into the trees.

"Did you get him," Vanessa asked.

A black figure suddenly swooped down and knocked Claus into a tree. It was so fast that Vanessa couldn't even catch a glimpse before it retreated back into the trees.

"It's so fast," Vanessa said.

Claus couldn't see. He sat down by the tree.

"Sir," Chad said. He ran over to Claus.

Claus' arm was bleeding.

The figure dived toward Vanessa and Chad.

"It's coming back," Vanessa yelled. She held her staff up.

"That's a different staff," Chad said.

"Inferio," Vanessa shouted. Her staff was crackling with energy. She threw her staff. It struck the figure.

The figure screeched and zoomed off.

Chad wrapped a rag around Claus' arm.

"Is he okay," Vanessa asked.

"Yes," Chad said. "I'll take him to the hospital and you go tell Professor Ludas."

"Okay."

Minutes later, Vanessa was outside Professor Ludas' office door. She heard some yelling, so she put her ear at the door.

"You can't just let her continue this charade," Professor Suna yelled.

"I know it isn't her," Professor Ludas shouted back.

"The pieces all fit," Professor Suna cried.

"What are they talking about," Vanessa wondered.

"Ssh," Professor Suna said. "Our conversation is no longer private."

The door flew open and revealed a curious Vanessa.

Professor Suna rushed out of the room.

"Vanessa, what is it," Professor Ludas asked. He leaned over his cauldron and held his head.

"Claus is hurt. A monster attacked us at detention," Vanessa cried.

"Is he in the hospital," Professor Ludas asked.

Vanessa nodded. "Chad took him."

Professor Ludas sighed in relief. "Good, thank you. Please go to your room."

"But, sir," Vanessa said.

"Do as I say, Vanessa," Professor Ludas shouted.

"I can't! What is that creature that attacked us; I want to know," Vanessa shouted. "Was it Evangeline?"

Professor Ludas took his staff out.

Vanessa thought her was going to attack her, but instead a clear stream of light appeared around Professor Ludas' head. It appeared to have become a manifestation of the events that just happened.

"I think it is best if you just vast them away, like a gentle breeze," Professor Ludas said.

Chapter XIV:

The Vampire Breath's Owner

The next day went by slowly as Vanessa held Chad, Beverly, Jackson, Poliy, and Grace inside the huge library. They were looking for clues to as of what Vanessa and Chad had encountered the night before. Vanessa was determined to find the truth of what was going on.

Beverly dropped into a chair. "I can't find anything," she said.

"Me, either," Poliy added. He sighed. "We've been looking all day."

"To tell the truth, I didn't look that hard," Grace said, floating around Beverly's head.

"I kind of figured that," Vanessa said.

"Come on, Vanessa. You've to give us more details," Jackson said.

"I can't remember too much," Vanessa snapped.

"Calm down, guys," Beverly said. "We won't get anywhere like this."

"She's right," Poliy said.

Chad suddenly threw a huge book on to the table, which made everyone jump.

"What's that," Grace asked.

"This book is about vampires," Chad replied. "It's more likely that it was a vampire that night that attacked us."

"Chad, what is with you and your suspicions of vampires," Vanessa asked.

"I know," Beverly said.

"Look at the clues, you idiots: blood sucking and only attacking on the New Moon," Chad said.

"It probably is a vampire, you know," Jackson said. "Vanessa, you said that Ms. Norris is missing a bottle of vampire breath, didn't you?"

"So," Vanessa said.

"What is vampire breath, anyway," Beverly asked.

"I think it's a fang," Chad said.

"Yes. Vampire breath is a mist that some witches and wizards trap in a bottle; it is actually just a vampire's fangs," Poliy explained.

"It's just that the vampire breath is a precaution to help a vampire stop craving."

"It must be a vampire," Jackson said.

"Attacking on a New Moon, it must be a half demon," Chad said. "Half vampires are the main ones who attack on the New Moon since the others attack at any time."

Poliy suddenly got all big eyed.

"What's wrong," Grace asked.

"Vanessa, do you think it could be Evangeline," Poliy asked. "She is half demon, remember?"

"Evangeline was acting strange during the test, looking at the moon," Jackson said.

"No, don't say that," Vanessa shouted. She teared up.

"Vanessa, remember what you and Evangeline talked about? Maybe that thing is making Evangeline act like this," Poliy said.

"What," Jackson asked.

"Well, Evangeline had been hearing voices recently just like me," Vanessa said.

"Voices? Maybe it's her other half tempting her but I don't know what you could be hearing," Chad exclaimed.

"It could be a demon," Poliy said.

Vanessa didn't want to believe it. She had to find out the truth.

"We shouldn't jump to conclusions. Why don't we ask Evangeline ourselves?" Grace asked.

Vanessa sprinted out of the library and down the corridor. "It can't be true! Could it?" she thought. Almost tripping over a flight of stairs, Vanessa busted into Evangeline's room, almost tearing down the door.

Evangeline and Dominus were standing next to the window. Evangeline quickly threw a small, glass bottle on the bed, and Dominus smothered it with a pillow.

"What was that," Vanessa asked.

"I was trying some perfume on," Evangeline replied.

"Do you wish to say something," Dominus asked Vanessa.

"Evangeline, if I asked you something would you tell me the truth," Vanessa asked. She slowly walked towards Evangeline with fear in eyes. She noticed that Evangeline's eyes were bloodshot.

"Yes, I wouldn't lie to, Vanessa. You know that," Evangeline said. She started grinding her teeth.

Vanessa rolled her eyes away.

"What is wrong," Evangeline asked.

"Well, I know it's a stupid question but, I know that you're a vampire but are you the one attacking people," Vanessa asked.

Evangeline twitched once very quickly.

"Are you alright," Vanessa asked.

"Of course not. You know that," Evangeline said.

"Vanessa, where'd this come from," Dominus asked.

"We were looking in books inside the library and…," Vanessa said.

Just then, Beverly waltzed into the room. "Sorry, I'm intruding, aren't I," she asked.

Vanessa glanced at Evangeline. Seeing she was getting annoyed, Vanessa decided to leave. "I was just leaving." She and Beverly left the room and closed the door behind them.

"Did she tell you," Beverly asked.

"She said she isn't," Vanessa said.

"But there are so many clues," Beverly said.

"Where's everyone else," Vanessa asked.

"They went by their own business," Beverly replied.

Vanessa sighed. "Maybe Evangeline is the vampire."

"There isn't any other proof," Beverly said.

"Wait, she had a little bottle. She claims it was perfume," Vanessa said.

"We should sneak in her room and see if it's the vampire breath," Beverly said.

"But she'll be in her room. How will we get in," Vanessa asked.

"We'll need a distraction," Beverly said.

"A distraction, huh?" Vanessa said.

"Yeah," Beverly said.

"Wait, let's try something else. Who else does she trust?" Beverly said. "Her Magica Dominus, Dominus, right?"

"How can we get Dominus out and turn into her," Vanessa asked.

"Pookie'll know," Beverly said.

"Who," Vanessa asked.

"Jackson," Beverly said.

"You nicknamed him Pookie," Vanessa asked. "That's really lame."

"There's nothing wrong with being lame," Beverly said. "Let's go get Jackson. He's the only one that stayed in the library."

"Do we really need him? I don't want everyone to know," Vanessa said.

Beverly sighed. "Just be here tonight. Leave everything to me."

Vanessa frowned at the idea to deceive her own sister, but she felt she had the right to know.

That night after the suits of armor made their rounds around the castle, Vanessa quickly ventured throughout the halls and stopped right beside Evangeline's door. "Where's Beverly?" Vanessa wanted to do this and get finished.

Suddenly, Dominus appeared beside Vanessa.

Vanessa gasped. "Dominus!"

"It's me," Dominus said in Beverly's voice.

"Beverly," Vanessa said. "You transformed into Dominus."

"Jackson, gave me the spell to change into someone else," Beverly said.

"Where's the real Dominus," Vanessa asked.

"I got Poliy to take him outside," Beverly said.

Just then, Vanessa heard whispering. "Ssh." She put her ear to the door.

"What is it," Beverly asked.

"Evangeline's talking to someone," Vanessa said.

Evangeline was talking and Vanessa also heard the same voice that she had heard before.

Vanessa's eyes glowed green.

"What's wrong, 'nessa?"

Vanessa busted the door open. She and Beverly ran in but saw no one.

"Huh," Beverly said.

Vanessa noticed the open window. "Tell Poliy to come after me," she said. She took out her staff and got on it.

"Wait, where are you going," Beverly asked.

"After Evangeline," Vanessa replied.

"Why," Beverly asked.

"There's something after my sister!" Vanessa said. She zoomed out of the window on her staff.

"Come back," Beverly shouted.

Vanessa hovered above the forest. "Where'd she go?" Out of the corner of her eye, Vanessa noticed Evangeline darting through the brick road, leading toward the entrance of the school. Vanessa dived

toward Evangeline. "Is it really her?" She flew through the forest and she could clearly see a figure in a black robe. "Stop!"

The figure stopped running on the brick road.

Vanessa jumped off her staff. "Who are you?!"

The figure threw a young boy down.

Vanessa noticed his neck was red. "His neck. You're a vampire," Vanessa said.

The figure pulled its robe off. It was Evangeline!

"Evangeline," Vanessa said.

"Or Harpy," Evangeline added. She looked down and frowned. "I didn't want you to see me like this."

Chapter XV:

Magic and the Dark Arts

"Evangeline," Vanessa said.

"I guess you've finally found out," Evangeline said. "I guess you didn't get the kind of sister you wanted, huh?"

"I get it now. Professor Suna told Professor Ludas about what you were doing, but he didn't believe it," Vanessa said.

"But why wouldn't he," Evangeline asked.

Vanessa paused for a moment. "The vampire breath. He thought your breath was locked in the library," she said. "And you were the one drinking the animal's blood."

"I'm afraid it's all true," Evangeline said. "I stole my breathe from the library."

"Why, Evangeline? Weren't you doing well until now? What happened," Vanessa asked.

"I was hungry," Evangeline shouted. "I'm not like you. I'm a monster, don't you understand? Blood is so tempting!"

"No, you're just different. Being different is good," Vanessa said.

"You guys don't understand," Evangeline yelled. "Only one person understands."

"What's wrong with you," Vanessa asked. "And who's this one person?"

"Just leave me alone. You are just in the way," Evangeline said. "He told me that you're just an insect compared to me."

"Who," Vanessa asked.

Evangeline put her cloak back on and soared into the air.

"She has no staff, but she can fly," Vanessa said amazed. She got on her staff and zoomed after Evangeline through the courtyard.

Evangeline looked back. "She's fast; in a few years, she may specialize in flying. Interesting," she thought.

"Evangeline, wait. I don't get it," Vanessa shouted. "I thought we had a connection now. What did I do?"

Evangeline circled the top of the school.

"I can't take her back if she doesn't stop. I'll have to take her back by force," Vanessa said. She held her hand out and yelled, "Windoa!" Six clones of Vanessa appeared and flew toward Evangeline.

"Wind clones from a first year? The brat may make me work," Evangeline said. She swung her arm and a giant blade of purple energy shot out of it and destroyed the clones.

"Oh, no," Vanessa said. "My clones!"

"What's wrong, Vanessa? Didn't inherit mommy's magical powers?" Evangeline asked.

Vanessa grunted. "I have to stop her," Vanessa said. She sped up toward Evangeline. "If I can just get the cloak." She reached for the tip end of Evangeline's cloak.

"As if you could," Evangeline said.

Vanessa couldn't catch up to Evangeline. She felt her grip loosening on her staff. "I can't hold on," she said.

Evangeline glared at Vanessa and grinned. She kicked Vanessa in the face causing Vanessa to lose her grip completely.

Vanessa groaned and started falling. She crashed on top of the school roof. Her back felt like it was split in two.

Evangeline landed next to Vanessa. She kicked Vanessa's arm.

"Stop!" Vanessa said. "Oww."

"What's your problem? Why won't you leave me alone," Evangeline yelled.

Vanessa stared at Evangeline. "Tell me what happened to you."

"You want to know that badly, don't you," Evangeline asked.

"You're my sister. I want to know everything about you," Vanessa said. "Is that voice making you do this?"

"I'll tell you, if you can take me back by force. Why don't you try casting your spell again?" Evangeline said.

"Okay. Cro--," Vanessa said. She held her staff out.

Suddenly, Dominus dropped out of the sky and roosted in front of Vanessa. He flicked Vanessa on the forehead with her wing, which made her stop saying her spell.

"Crap," Vanessa said. "Huh." "Where's Poliy?"

"Are you scared," Evangeline asked. "Think you can't handle this situation by yourself? You have to learn to do things on your own."

Dominus looked at Vanessa with worried eyes. "Evangeline, stop it. She is only worried about you."

Evangeline frowned and scoffed. "Now you are taking her side? Really? Can I not have anybody stay with me?"

"You know it's not like that," Vanessa shouted. She struggled to her feet.

"You don't know anything about being alone. You've been loved, and you have had someone protecting you your whole life," Evangeline shouted back. "Shut up. You piss me off, acting like you know me."

Vanessa grunted. "But I want to."

"What does that mean," Evangeline asked. "What is companionship going to do for me at this point. I'm nothing but a monster that has no place in this world." She wiped her blood-stained mouth. "Dominus."

Dominus grabbed Vanessa by the neck. "I am sorry, but I must do what Evangeline says."

Vanessa moaned.

"And now I will fulfill the demon's dream. Once I bite you, I will be a full-fledged vampire and have a place where I belong," Evangeline said.

"What does that have to do with me," Vanessa said, gasping for air.

"I found out in order to become a full Harpy, I must suck a large quantity of blood from a related sibling," Evangeline explained.

"No," Vanessa said. Vanessa's eyes started to tear up and her vision was blurry. She saw an unusual black orb circling around Evangeline.

"Now, Evangeline. Get the blood you have wanted for so long," a raspy voice said.

"Who is that," Vanessa asked.

Evangeline put her lips on Vanessa's neck.

"Do it," the voice said. "You will be the one that starts the Harpy muck again."

Evangeline started to breathe heavily. "I can't do it," she said.

"Why can't you," the raspy voice yelled.

"She's my sister," Evangeline said.

"Sister," the voice said angrily.

"Not even a sister. She is me. I can't do it," Evangeline said. "I could leave her enough blood to keep her alive so I would stay alive,

but what would be the point? I don't want to be alone anymore; I would be doing the exact same thing to her."

Dominus let go of Vanessa.

Vanessa slid off the roof and hung on the edge of a strong, rusty nail. She was unconscious at this point.

"You can't do this now. What about all that we've been through, the planning we've done?" the voice said.

"That is my flesh and blood. You got into my mind. Normally, I would have never even thought about hurting Vanessa, certainly because of my condition," Evangeline said.

"Evangeline," Dominus said. She picked Vanessa up by the collar of her shirt with his beak.

"Leave us alone," Evangeline yelled at the black orb.

"Damn, you, winch," the voice said.

Vanessa opened her eyes and groaned. "Evangeline?"

Evangeline looked at Vanessa. "Get out of here, Vanessa," she yelled.

"Evangeline, what's that," Vanessa asked, pointing at the black orb.

"I don't exactly know, but it was controlling my mind. I know its evil; that's why I'm going to send back to where it came from," Evangeline replied.

"Fool, I am a demon," the orb said. "You know me better than anyone, Evangeline."

"Demon?" Vanessa said.

The orb turned into a naked, light skinned man with blond hair. His hair was dirty and his body was covered in burn marks.

"Hibiki," Evangeline said. She gasped.

"This is my form before my life was changed by the devil," the man said.

"The devil," Vanessa yelled.

The man gazed at Vanessa. "You. You just had to get rid of the Drainage, didn't you? How did it take that long to even drain your power?"

"How do you know about that," Vanessa asked.

"Fool, my master was using you to get to Evangeline. If we drained your magic, we could use it to gain more control over Evangeline," the man said.

"You bastard," Evangeline yelled. She started running toward the man, but Dominus quickly pulled her back with his claw. As soon as she did, a giant, blue wave of magic hit the man.

The man fell to his knees.

Professor Ludas suddenly came falling from the sky. He landed next to Vanessa, Evangeline, and Dominus.

"Daddy," Evangeline said.

Professor Ludas smiled at her. "Girls, get back. I'm about to send him back to Hell," Professor Ludas said.

"Heh, think about it, Evangeline. Do you want to stay here, where you'll get no better than you are," the man said. "The devil could help you with that if you're nice."

"Evangeline, don't go," Vanessa said. She got on her knees and tears started to run down her cheeks.

Evangeline glared at Vanessa.

"You are my sister and a friend. You don't know how much it meant to me when you started talking tom me, acknowledging me," Vanessa said.

"Vanessa," Dominus said.

"I'll do anything. Just don't go," Vanessa said. She grabbed on to Evangeline's shoes.

Evangeline kneeled down and wiped the tears from Vanessa's cheeks.

"A bond is what you two have. I'll just have to sever that bond," the man said.

Chapter XVI:

The Bond is United

The man held his hand up toward Professor Ludas. "Eva baby."

"Eva baby," Vanessa thought. "Where have I heard that before?"

"Look out," Evangeline yelled.

A giant flame emerged from the man's hand and shot at Professor Ludas.

Professor Ludas galloped around to avoid the flames. "Kids, run!" He tripped and fell off of the roof.

"Dominus," Evangeline said.

"Yes," Dominus said. He dived off of the roof and grabbed Professor Ludas, beak clamped onto Luda's staff.

"Why do you want Evangeline so badly," Vanessa asked.

"Evangeline is a demon such as me. She should come with us in the underworld," the man said. "She would be a great addition to our ranks."

"I'm not going anywhere," Evangeline said.

"I beg the differ," the man said. "Give in to the power, Evangeline. You know you want to." He grinned.

Evangeline suddenly felt a sharp pain in her head again. She fell to the ground, kicking, and screaming. "Get out of my head!"

Vanessa ran over to Evangeline and held her. "Evangeline, tell me what's wrong!" She stared at the man. "Who are you?!"

"I'm upset that you don't not know me. I think I'll leave," the man said. He disappeared.

Evangeline suddenly stopped struggling and screaming.

"What's wrong now," Vanessa asked.

Evangeline stood up and grabbed Vanessa by the throat. He eyes were pure black. "Vanessa, he released my demon," Evangeline said. "I don't have control over my body."

Vanessa groaned. "Fight it," she said. She couldn't breathe.

Evangeline chuckled and threw Vanessa.

Vanessa flew off of the roof and crashed into a giant boulder next to the forest. Her staff fell into a ditch.

"Let's see if you're better than me; can you use magic without your staff?" Evangeline said.

Vanessa blacked out again.

Dominus grunted and looked at Evangeline. "Evangeline…"

"Don't fall asleep," Evangeline yelled. She jumped off of the roof of the school and charged toward Vanessa.

"Master, no," Dominus yelled.

"I know if I kill you, it'll kill me, but I have to know which of us is meant to live and be the real version," Evangeline said. She kicked Vanessa in the stomach and slapped her with her staff.

Vanessa spit up blood and coughed.

Evangeline held Vanessa's limp body up by the hair. She gave a devilish grin.

Suddenly, deep inside Vanessa, a mystic power was boiling. A green energy swirled around her.

Evangeline sensed the change and quickly let go of Vanessa and jumped back. "What is that?"

A stench started coming from Vanessa. A gruesome voice called out to her "Grr."

"Evangeline, please stop," Professor Ludas said. He tried to stand, but fell back into Dominus' enormous wing due to the pain.

Vanessa lay motionless on the ground.

"You… you pitiful witch. You are weak, aren't you?" the gruesome voice said. "I thought I'd be able to live within you peacefully, but it seems that won't happen. You've been causing trouble since you started using magic. Damn it. Consider this taste of my power, a piece of delicious cake. You should be grateful that I'm here, child."

Vanessa suddenly got to her feet and was consumed deeper into the green light.

"This aura! Whose magic is that?" Professor Ludas grunted.

Suddenly, the aura became even stronger and pinned Evangeline down to the ground. Professor Ludas and Dominus were also pinned. They could not move.

"This magic is overwhelming," Evangeline said. She struggled to her feet. "What is this?"

Vanessa opened her eyes. Her eyes had turned pure black as well. She ran toward Evangeline, grabbed her, and threw her into the air. "Evangeline, you are coming back, even if I have to break every bone in your body!" Vanessa held her hand out.

Evangeline's body started to ache. It felt like every bone in her body was breaking and crumbling under the magical pressure. She screamed and slammed into the wall of the school.

Vanessa started foaming from her mouth and twisted her neck. She was not the Vanessa we all knew. Her fingernails grew longer and her hair turned blonder.

Evangeline dug herself out of the wall and a pair of dark, giant bat wings sprouted from her back. She let out an ear shattering screech.

Vanessa growled and charged toward Evangeline.

"Vanessa, no! What is going on?" Pro. Ludas yelled.

"Vanessa, I see now. You are very special; but you see, you're not the only special one," Evangeline said. She opened her wings and flew toward Vanessa. "I want you to feel the loneliness I felt for all those years. You got to have family reunions, Christmases, and birthday parties!"

"I don't understand," Dominus said.

"Evangeline is being influenced by the demon inside of her. Only her heart can regain control," Professor Ludas explained.

"Vanessa is trying to knock some sense into her, but I don't understand what has happened to her."

As Evangeline and Vanessa drew closer to each other, an eerie silence fell over them.

Vanessa suddenly stopped running and Evangeline ran into her arms. Vanessa hugged her tightly.

"She stopped," Dominus said in awe.

Vanessa fell asleep, and as she did, Evangeline's wings vanished.

"It's over," Professor Ludas said. He sighed. "Dominus, please put me down."

Dominus placed him on the ground.

A warm, gently breeze flew across Vanessa's face. She awoke in a comfortable bed inside the hospital wing. She looked across the room and saw Poliy in another bed. Vanessa sat up and rubbed her eyes. "How'd I get here? What happened?"

"Knock, knock," Evangeline said.

"May we come in," Professor Ludas asked. Both he and Evangeline walked into the room.

"Oh," Vanessa said. "You guys are ok. Was that just a dream?"

"No dream," Evangeline replied. She showed her fangs.

"You know, it's very good to be respectful," Professor Ludas said.

"Vanessa, how are you," Evangeline asked.

"Fine. What happened?" Vanessa said.

"Well, you.. you hugged Evangeline and that broke her demon's control," Professor Ludas explained.

"I don't understand," Vanessa said.

"Love and compassion are the only things that could drive the demon back inside of me," Evangeline said. She blushed and folded her arms.

"Hey, are you all right now," Vanessa asked.

"More or less," Evangeline said.

"If you don't mind me asking, Evangeline, who was that man," Vanessa asked.

Evangeline looked confused. "That was our dad, well your dad but you know what I mean."

Vanessa gasped. "What the heck?! He's a demon?"

"It's a long story that your mother will have to fill you in on another day," Pro. Ludas exclaimed.

Vanessa never imagined meeting her dad this way. She frowned. "Evangeline, since we are being honest. Who was that rat?" "

Harold? My old Magica Dominus," Evangeline said. She pouted and wanted to change the subject.

"What happened to him? How did you end up with Dominus," Vanessa asked?

"Harold was killed, trying to protect me. I used to live in a village with Professor Ludas, but one day, they found out that I was a vampire and wanted to drive a stake through my heart," Evangeline explained.

Vanessa felt that she should not ask anymore.

"That's all I can tell you now," Evangeline said, trying not to cry.

Pro. Ludas hugged her.

"Vanessa, what was that power that engulfed you?" asked Pro. Ludas.

Vanessa looked at her hands and started to sweat. I don't know."

"I know what it was," Pro. Suna said while walking into the room.

"Professor," Vanessa said.

"You looked into it like I asked," Pro. Ludas asked.

Pro. Suna nodded. "It is known as the Levia Spirit: a spirit made of the combined essence of dark magical and light magical energy."

"A spirit?" Poliy said. He sat up in the bed. "Interesting."

"When did you get up," Vanessa asked.

"Just did," Poliy replied. "Where did it come from?"

"Levia Spirits are known to just roam the world with no particular destination. They used to be regarded as demons themselves but they are neither demonic or heavenly beings. They are an anomaly."

Vanesa gulped. "Is it ok for it to be inside of me?"

"Well, you never knew it was there before," Poliy said.

"True. Just think of it as an ally. Since it resides inside of you, you being its host makes it vulnerable; if you die, it dies too so it will give you a much-needed push in magical pressure," Pro. Ludas said.

"So that was the power I felt," Evangeline said. "Amazing."

Vanessa stared at herself in the mirror.

"Sorry for the trouble," Evangeline said to Poliy.

"It's cool, sweet cakes," Poliy said.

Evangeline growled at him.

"Evangeline, were you intimidated by me? Wasn't your demon side trying to find out who was stronger," Vanessa asked.

Evangeline frowned and looked away. "I'm sorry. If anything I should be explain our dad."

"I... I just couldn't help noticing the few similarities that he had with Evangeline and me," Vanessa said.

"Evangeline is the right one to tell you," Professor Ludas said.

"Tell me what?" Vanessa said.

Evangeline grunted. She wiped the tears from her eyes. "He sold his soul to the devil."

"No wonder. I'm kind of glad I didn't know him, or I would have gotten attached to him and this would hurt more," Vanessa said.

"I know what you mean," Evangeline said.

Vanessa felt that everyone needed a pick me up. "So, what's today," Vanessa asked.

"Well, actually, it's the last day of school," Evangeline said, brightly.

"Your mom is waiting for you downstairs. Both of you," Professor Ludas said.

"You mean it? I can stay?" Evangeline asked.

"Huh," Vanessa asked.

Professor Ludas smiled. "Evangeline wants to spend the break with you and your mom."

Evangeline hugged him.

Vanessa jumped out of the bed and shrieked.

"All well that ends well," Poliy said. "Feels like someone's said that already."

Vanessa stopped celebrating. "Where's everyone else?" Vanessa asked.

"Outside with mom," Evangeline said. "Come on, Vanessa. Let's go home." She held her hand out for Vanessa.

And as Vanessa jumped out of bed as if it were Christmas Day, she felt her empty heart suddenly fill with the joy and companionship of those around her. Without noticing it or really trying to figure it out, Vanessa had actually found what she'd been looking for all along: a sense of belonging in her sister's heart.

Thank you for reading it to the end! If you enjoyed this book, please look out for the next entry: Vanessa Owens and the Book of Reality. It'll be coming out soon. Again, thank you.

www.ingramcontent.com/pod-product-compliance
Lightning Source LLC
Chambersburg PA
CBHW030336180626
46810CB00003B/1379